WADE IN THE WATER

WADE IN THE WATER
▼

Nathaniel A. Lumpkin II

Writers Club Press
San Jose New York Lincoln Shanghai

Wade in the Water

All Rights Reserved © 2001 by Nathaniel A. Lumpkin II

No part of this book may be reproduced or transmitted in any form or by any means, graphic, electronic, or mechanical, including photocopying, recording, taping, or by any information storage retrieval system, without the permission in writing from the publisher.

Writers Club Press
an imprint of iUniverse.com, Inc.

For information address:
iUniverse.com, Inc.
5220 S 16th, Ste. 200
Lincoln, NE 68512
www.iuniverse.com

ISBN: 0-595-13625-7

Printed in the United States of America

This book is dedicated to the loving memory of my dear sister Gail and my father Nathaniel Lumpkin Sr.

Acknowledgements

I give all the honor, glory and praise to God, for giving me the creativeness and ability to write this book. I'm eternally grateful to my beautiful wife Karen for her understanding and support during the entire process, I love you babe. And I would not be the man I am today if it were not for my mother, Kathyren, whom always believed in me and has always been a big support in all my past endeavors, I love you too mom. I also want to thank my in laws, Doris and Jesse for their kind and thoughtful support. And last but certainly not least, I want to acknowledge my three beautiful children, Mariah, Breanna and Nathaniel III. Thank you for being the blessings that you are and for making my life so fullfilling, I love you more than words can say.

Contents

Chapter 1 Friendship 1

Chapter 2 Colored Gal 12

Chapter 3 Midnight 16

Chapter 4 God's Creatures 24

Chapter 5 The Angel Appears 27

Chapter 6 Friendly Relations 41

Chapter 7 Vanished 47

Chapter 8 The Surprise 51

Chapter 9 College 61

Chapter 10 Welcome Home 67

Chapter 11 Mary Houston 72

Chapter 12 The Rape 91

Chapter 13 New Lessons 104

Chapter 14 The Trial 115

Chapter 15 Prison Bound 136

Chapter 16 Life 144

Chapter 17 The Confession 154

Chapter 18 I'm Negro American, I'm Angry and I'm Here 162
Chapter 19 Now Comes Freedom 170
Chapter 20 Home Sweet Home 174

Chapter 1

Friendship

Sitting here under the bright blue southern skies of Georgia, on these red banks of the Ginsburg river, swatting flies and swamped by unbearable heat and humidity, I'm enjoying the first day of freedom in nearly twenty years. Not much has changed in this place we called New Bethlehem, a place not likely to be found on any maps, it was quite simply, the colored part of town. It was a place as lush and green as any Irish village, filled with life and adventure. The cotton fields looked like snow in the spring time and the small homes dotting the country side is where hard working families lived and thrived at a time most thought impossible.

This old river is still red and muddy and the smell of those sweet Georgia pines is like peach cobbler to me. I can still hear the sound of the choir as it echoes through the woods, and that old church is just as I had imagined it would be, and if I concentrate real hard I can almost hear my momma calling me in for supper. My earliest childhood memories was when I was eight or nine years old. I was a skinny, nappy head colored boy back then, my skin was dark and I was always ashey. My summer days were spent reading books and fishing without a care in the world, most of the time.

As I sit here reminiscing on my childhood, I remember it was a mixture of both good and bad memories, one shaping the other and inseparable. My past helped to shape who I would become but it did not determine who I am. I was the fifth son and youngest child of nine, living in a black and white world that was full of all the vibrant colors of the rainbow. We lived in a old three bedroom farm house that my daddy built. The walls of that old house were made out of wooden planks from the rail yard and they were held together with crooked, rusty nails. My momma and daddy had their own room while the girls shared another room and one bed between them. My four older brothers and I shared the other room, and just like my sisters we too shared one bed.

I didn't take up to much space so it wasn't that uncomfortable, especially because it was all I knew. That old house wasn't much to look at but we called it home, and if those rooms had a voice the stories they'd tell would speak volumes. My daddy was a sharecropper and his skin was black as coal from working his whole life out in that scorching sun. He was a big man and some folks say he was as strong as a mule. Daddy believed in standing his ground and speaking his mind. That was extremely dangerous for a colored man to do in those days but my daddy wasn't afraid of no man, or nothing.

My momma cleaned white folks house's and cooked their meals. She was a thin, beautiful, light skinned woman with long brown hair that seemed to flow like a river. She had a small mole on her right temple and she called it her beauty mark. Momma was also a very spiritual woman, unyielding in the things of God and just as unwavering. The folks in New Bethlehem used to say that momma looked too young to have had nine children and that's a fact, she was pretty enough to be in one of those Hollywood picture shows. I once heard my momma pray to the good Lord, and she asked Him to send down a heavenly Angel to watch over all her youngins, and I believe He did just that.

Times were hard back then and all of us youngins had to share clothes, shoes and pretty much anything else you could think of.

Growing up in a family of eleven we couldn't afford to be selfish, and we learned the importance of giving and sharing early in life. We all had jobs to do around the farm. My brothers and sisters had to work with my daddy in the fields but not me, my job was to stay in school. When I wasn't in school I used to tote fresh drinking water and food out to them in the fields. Around the farm I took care of the chickens, hogs and daddy's old mule. My daddy wanted me to stay in school and get an education. He used to tell folks that I was smart as a whip and he also said I wasn't made for farm work because I was too scrawny. All the colored children went to school in the church and Reverend Hightower was our teacher. He was a heavy set light skinned colored man with green eyes to match. The Reverend was so light I suppose if he wanted to he could pass for a white man, but as far as I knew he never did.

At the end of every school year Reverend Hightower would ring the church bell and all the colored boys and girls would take off running home as fast as they could, but I grabbed my fishing pole that I kept on the side of the church and went fishing. I spent the first few years of my life as a loner with no real friends to speak of because all the other colored children went to work in the fields with their families after school. I was accustomed to spending my time alone but little did I know that that was about to change forever. It was the summer of 1923, a warm, peaceful afternoon, not much different than today. I could hear the harmonious sounds of the birds singing in the trees, which was music to my ears, and the leaves brushing against one another in the breeze sounded like God's own symphony.

I was reading a book about Benjamin Banneker which so consumed me, that I could envision his face and his amazing accomplishments. My fishing pole was planted in the ground beside me and the line was cast into the river searching for an unsuspecting catfish that was to be my family's entree. My peaceful existence was suddenly disturbed by a loud scream and a splash in the water. I stood up to see what had caused that splash but to my surprise there was nothing. I stood there puzzled for a moment as the water slowly stopped making waves. I was very curious so I slowly began to wade in the water to see what I could see, then suddenly and without any warning, a skinny, blond haired, blue eyed white boy came up out of that water like a fish and yelled, "Boo." I turned around and got out of that water so fast, I probably would have still been running today if I hadn't heard that white boy laughing his fool head off. I stopped running and turned around to see what he was laughing at. I paused for a moment, then realized he was laughing at me. I thought about how funny I must have looked, then I started laughing right along with him. We fell down on that muddy bank and laughed ten or fifteen minutes, during which time we introduced ourselves to one another.

"What's yo name?" he asked with a deep southern drawl.

"Jeremiah," I said.

"What's yours?"

"Billy Ray," he said.

"What choo doin round here Billy Ray, don't no white chirin live round here?"

"My daddy bought all dis land," he said.

"Mr. Horton own dis here land," I said.

"I know dat, cause he's my uncle, I'm Billy Ray Horton."

"You mean yo daddy bought dis land from his own brother?"

"Well, not exactly, my uncle owes my daddy allot of money, but on account of he can't pay him, my daddy took his land as payment. My uncle got real mad and dey cursed each other, but he finally gave my daddy da papers."

"My daddy work dis land all his life, Mr. Horton say one day he gonna sell my daddy some land so he can go into farmin fo his self," I said.

"Well, I don't think my daddy gonna sell dis land, he's up to the house now making all kinds of plans, kissing my new momma and spinning her round in circles and such."

"So does dat mean my daddy work for yo daddy now?"

"I reckon so."

I sat there thinking about my daddy and how hard he worked and all the promises Mr. Horton made to him. Every couple of weeks my daddy got up before sunrise and put some white poison in a cloth bag, and walked every other row of those two hundred acres shaking that bag over the cotton to poison the bow weevil, then he worked in those fields until sundown and sometimes he worked under the moon light. I remember one time during cotton season my daddy worked so hard his hands were covered with blood because the bolls around the cotton were sharp enough to cut paper. Many days my daddy came home too sleepy to talk and too tired to eat. During that time all he wanted to do was close his eyes. I remember one day I asked my daddy why he worked so hard on somebody else's land. He said, "Ya'll got to eat don't choo? Ya'll need shoes and clothes don't choo? Besides, one day we gonna own dis land, dat's why."

I thought long and hard about what my daddy said. I heard stories about colored folks that owned their own land I just never seen any of them, but I suppose my daddy thought he'd be the first.

"Hey Jeremiah, you wanna see a gold pocket watch and chain?"

"Yea!" I said. "Where'd choo get dat Billy Ray?"

"My daddy gave it to me."

"Is it real gold?"

"Yep!"

"I ain't never seen a gold pocket watch and chain up close, can I touch it?"

"Sure, you can put it in yo pocket if you have a mind to."

"This sho is a fine watch, yo daddy must be rich," I said with admiration.

"I reckon!"

"How yo daddy get so rich anyway?"

"I ain't supposed to tell."

"Why? Is it a secret?"

"Somethin like dat!"

"You can trust me Billy Ray, I won't tell nobody, I promise."

"Well,,,you promise and hope to die if'n you tell?"

"I promise and hope to die if'n I tell!"

"My daddy sells corn liquor."

"Moonshine?" I said surprisingly. "Ain't dat against da law Billy Ray?"

"I suppose so, dat's why my daddy would skin me alive if'n he knew I told you!"

"But how can he get rich selling moonshine?"

"My daddy got a whole buncha still's all over da county. Some folks pay allot a money fo my daddy's corn liquor, even sheriff Banks."

"Da sheriff? But he's da sheriff, he's supposed to up hold da law," I said.

Well, I suppose he can do what ever he want since he's da sheriff," said Billy Ray.

I was never so shocked in all my short life. Looking back in retrospect, I don't know why I was so surprised, white folks always did do what ever they wanted to do, no matter who it hurt or what the law said. We sat there for a while looking at the river, then Billy Ray came up with an idea.

"Hey Jeremiah do you want to go get some apples?"

"Where from?" I asked.

"I saw a whole buncha apple trees down Old Miller road."

"Naw, dem apple trees belong to Mr. Johnson," I said.

"So what, we won't get caught."

"But that'd be stealing, besides, Mr. Johnson got a big old shot gun and he'll shoot anybody he catch stealing his apples."

"Don't be a scary cat Jeremiah, we won't get caught."

Just as I was about to give in I heard a soft voice say *"don't do it."* I looked all around and I didn't see anyone except Billy Ray, but I knew what to say. "Naw, I betta not."

"Well, I'll be right back and I won't get caught, you'll see," he said.

Billy Ray took off down Old Miller road headed for Mr. Johnson's apple orchard while I stayed behind fishing. While Billy Ray was gone I must have caught three or four catfish. A short while later he came back to the river with a potato sack filled with green apples.

"I told choo I wouldn't get caught," he said with pride.

"Wow, how many apples did choo get?" I asked.

"I don't know, twenty or more I suppose."

"What choo gonna to do wit all dem apples Billy Ray?"

"Well, I can't eat all of em, do you want to take some home?"

"I don't know, my daddy might get mad if he thinks I stole em!"

"Jest tell him I gave em to you."

"Well, I don't know, naw, I betta not, you keep em Billy Ray."

"You really is a scary cat, Jeremiah."

"I ain't no scary cat, I jest don't want my daddy mad at me."

"What's he gonna get mad about, it's jest a bunch of apples?" he said.

"Well, maybe if I jest take a couple."

After Billy Ray gave me three or four apples I picked up my catfish, put my book in my back pocket and headed down the dirt road home. Half way down the road I got a little hungry so I started eating one of the apples. A few minutes later I saw a pretty colored gal walking down the road toward me. As we passed each other she smiled and said "hey." I said "hey" and kept on walking, not long after that I saw a big fat white man smoking a cigar coming toward me on a buck wagon. When he got right next to me he stopped the horse, and wouldn't you know it, it was Mr. Johnson. He was furious and he demanded to know where I got the apple I was eating.

"Where'd choo get dem apples boy?" he shouted.

I was so scared I didn't know what to do. I stood there with him yelling at me, unable to move and to afraid to talk. Mr. Johnson got down off the buckboard and snatched the bag of apples right out of my hand.

"Are you hard a hearing boy?" he yelled.
"No sir, I, I, I, I, I didn't steal dem apples sir!" I said with a stutter.
"These is my apples and I don't recall you paying for em."
"No sir, I, I, I, I, I didn't steal no apples sir, I, I, didn't steal em."
"Well, you gonna tell it to da sheriff boy."

Before I knew it Mr. Johnson grabbed me and threw me into the back of his wagon. My book about Benjamin Banneker fell out of my pocket and my catfish fell to the ground. Those catfish were still alive and they just flopped around on that dusty road without a drop of water or a frying pan in sight. Mr. Johnson took me to Burdonville, the town white folks lived in. There were all kinds of business's in Burdonville and at the time it was the only place I'd ever seen outside of New Bethlehem. There was a train station, post office, general store, livery stable, saloon, bank, jail and a hotel all down one street. As we rode through town I didn't know what was gonna happen, but I knew it wasn't gonna be good. It seemed like everybody stopped what they were doing and stared at me.

Colored folks and white folks alike were just shaking their heads like they knew something I didn't know. Maybe it was my imagination but they all looked like they had just come from a funeral. I heard stories about sheriff Banks and how he would take a whip and beat colored boys who got caught stealing and such. I heard a story one time about a colored boy from up north, who came down here to visit some of his kin folk and got caught smiling at a white girl. Well, shortly after that the sheriff and that white girls daddy whipped and beat that boy till he couldn't walk for a month. Sometime after that he went back up north and ain't never been back since.

While riding in the back of that wagon I had allot of time to think. If I told the sheriff where I got the apples he wouldn't believe me, besides, I might of gotten a beaten just for saying it was a white boy that stole them apples, even if it was the truth. I was so scared I just knew I might die. I thought about jumping off the back of that wagon and running off into the woods. But I heard that voice again telling me *"don't run and don't be afraid."* So I just sat there!

Besides, even if I did get away, Mr. Johnson might come looking for me then there would be all kinds of trouble because my daddy wouldn't let nobody put their hands on any of his family especially them white folks from Burdonville. So I just sat in the back of that wagon bouncing around like those catfish back on the road. I felt like the end was near and I wasn't ever gonna see my family again. When we arrived at the other end of town Mr. Johnson stopped that old horse of his and grabbed me by the back of my overalls and dragged me into the sheriffs office. I remember thinking that I should have kept on running when I met Billy Ray, instead, like a fool I turned back to wade in the water to see what caused that splash.

"Sheriff, sheriff, where are you?" yelled Mr. Johnson.

A few minutes later the sheriff came out. He was a hard looking man, unshaven, pot belly, and he looked like he hadn't had a bath in weeks. He was half dressed and more than likely he had been sleeping in his clothes. The office had empty bottles of moonshine all over the place and the trash can was over filled with crumbled up news papers. Before he even got close to me I could smell the liquor on his breath and all I could do was pray nobody struck a match.

"Why you making all dis racket Merle?" the sheriff grumbled.

"Sheriff, I caught dis boy stealing my apples and I want him punished."

"I didn't steal no apples sir," I said.

"You calling me a liar boy?" said Mr. Johnson.

"No sa, I ain't calling nobody no liar, sa."

"I caught dis boy eating my apples."

"Dat true boy," asked the sheriff.

"Yes sheriff, I was eaten a apple, but I didn't steal it."

"Well, if you didn't steal it, den where'd you get it from?" asked the sheriff.

"I'm telling you he stole it from my apple tree sheriff."

"Merle, will you jest shut up a minute."

"I jest want choo to punish dis boy for stealing my apples, dats all."

"Ain't choo Matthew Liggon's youngest boy?" asked the sheriff.

"Yes sa, I'm Jeremiah."

"Well Jeremiah, tell me da truth, where'd you get dem apples?"

"Well sa, they did come from Mr. Johnson's apple tree, but..."

"I told you sheriff, now give dat boy a lickin," said Mr. Johnson.

"Merle, I ain't gonna tell you again, shut up and let da boy finish talking."

At this time I was scared to death and I just knew if I told the truth I was dead for sure. While the sheriff was talking to Mr. Johnson I decided to tell them I took the apples, besides, they were gonna beat me either way I thought.

"Sheriff, I was eating Mr. Johnson's apples, but I didn't steal em."

"Well Jeremiah, if you didn't pay for em, den you stole em. So I tell you what I'm gonna do, I'm gonna take you to your daddy's farm and tell em what choo been up to. Den, you gonna work fer Merle in his apple orchard all day pickin apples till you pay em back, do you understand?"

"You mean you ain't gonna beat me sheriff?" I cried out.

"Now where'd you get a fool notion like dat?" asked the sheriff.

"I heard stories bout choo beaten colored boys till dey near dead for stealing."

"Well Jeremiah, don't believe everything you hear, but I do know one thang fo sho, yo daddy Matthew gonna beat da mess out choo fer gettin into trouble."

That sheriff was right, when I got home my daddy beat me so bad I didn't care if I ever saw another apple as long as I lived. I started working in Mr. Johnson's apple orchard the next day, and I ain't never ate another apple since. While I was standing on the ladder working, Billy Ray snuck up behind me and started shaking it. He made me drop all the apples I had just picked.

"Hey Jeremiah, what choo doing up there?"

"What do it look like Billy Ray?"

"Looks like you stealing some apples," he said laughingly.

"Hah, hah, hah very funny, Mr. Johnson caught me eatin a apple yesterday and he took me in to da sheriff's office."

"Did dey beat choo Jeremiah?" he asked with concern.

"Naw, dey didn't, but my daddy did, and now I got to work in these fields all day."

"Why didn't you jest tell em I stole dem apples?" asked Billy Ray.

"Cause I don't tell on my friends, besides, they don't take kindly to colored boys telling on white boys, don't choo know nothing?" I asked.

Billy Ray just stood there with a strange look on his face, I don't know if it was because I said I don't tell on my friends, or if it was because I took the blame for something he did. Either way, we became close and spent the rest of the summer together. That afternoon Billy Ray and I made a pact. We cut our right palms with my pocket knife and shook hands. We swore right then and there that we would always protect each other and always keep each other's secrets as long as we lived. Billy Ray worked with me all day picking apples and he didn't stop eating them. He was my first real friend and we shared allot of common interest, like most young boys I suppose.

Chapter 2

Colored Gal

The next day we made a raft and we pretended to be Captain Blye and Fletcher Christian. We made plans to sail the seven seas and discover new and exciting places together. The raft was tied to a tree so it wouldn't float down river, and we stood on it waving our wooden swords proclaiming victory against invisible pirates. We covered our heads with pieces of cloth and made eye patch's to look the part.

"I'm captain Blye," Billy Ray proclaimed. "And you are my first mate, Fletcher Christian."

"Why can't I be Captain Blye, and you be Fletcher Christian," I asked.

"Because Captain Blye was white, dat's why!"

"But so was Fletcher Christian, wasn't he!"

"I reckon so. Alright den, I'll be Fletcher Christian and you be Captain Blye."

It didn't seem to make that big of a difference to Billy Ray but it made a big difference to me. At the time I thought I could at least be the captain on our raggedy little raft, especially since I might never get the chance to be a real captain. We played on our ship and engaged ourselves in a little one on one battle, swinging our wooden swords at each other and breaking them in the process. As pieces of our swords fell into the river, we started to jump in and retrieve what was left, but we were halted by a shocking sight. The naked body of a colored girl was floating face down in the river, and she got stuck to the edge of our raft. Her hair was pulled back into a pony tail and there was no sign of life. We jumped off the raft onto the bank and ran as fast as we could to the church to tell Reverend Hightower.

"Reverend Hightower, Reverend Hightower," I yelled.

"Slow down, slow down boys. Now, what's all the excitement about?" he asked.

"There's a colored gal floating in da river, I think she's dead."

"Oh dear Lord. Show me where she is!" he said.

Reverend Hightower was to slow and over weight to keep up with us so we ran ahead to the river, but he kept us in sight. When we got back to the river she was gone. By the time the Reverend got to the river he was huffing and puffing so hard I thought he was gonna have a heart attack or something.

",,,,,,Where,,,,where is this dead gal boys?" he said as he tried to catch his breath.

"She was right there Reverend," I said.

"Do you know that the bible say's it is a sin to lie?"

"We ain't lying Reverend, she was right there when we came to tell you," said Billy Ray. "I swear it."

"We telling you da truth Reverend, she was right there a minute ago."

"Boys, when I was young I too had an over active imagination, but there is a time and a place for such things. Now, I'm a busy man and I don't have time to come running down here fooling wit you youngins and such, you hear?"

",,,,Yes sa!" I said reluctantly.

As the Reverend started walking back to the church that colored girls body floated to the surface.

"Reverend Hightower look," I said nervously. "There she is."

Reverend Hightower stopped in his tracks and started to raise his voice as he slowly turned around.

"I told you boys I don't have time to be fooling around wit you," he said. "Oh dear God," he said as he spotted the dead gal in the water. "Go get your daddy Jeremiah, and tell him to bring his wagon, hurry up now."

Me and Billy Ray took off running down Old Miller road toward my house to go get my daddy from the fields. By the time we got back Reverend Hightower had already pulled her out of the river and covered her with a blanket. The Reverend was cradling her in his arms and praying. My daddy told us to stay on the wagon and he got down and walked over to the Reverend and the dead gal.

"Who is she Reverend?" asked my daddy.

"I don't know Matthew, I ain't never seen this poor child before."

"Well where do you think she come from?"

"Up river most likely."

"What do you suppose happened to her Reverend?"

"Well, I don't rightly know. Maybe she drowned while she was swimming."

"Naw, she didn't drown Reverend, look at all those bruises on her neck, somebody killed this child."

"Wait a minute Matthew, those marks could have come from something in the water. She could have gotten hung up on anything down there. You and I both know there's all kinds of debris floating in this old river."

"Dat's true, but I done seen enough dead folk in my lifetime to know when dey been kilt."

"Well either way we have to tell sheriff Banks. Would you mind going into town to fetch him?"

"I'll go right now."

When my daddy came back to the wagon I saw the Reverend uncover the dead gals head and I could see her face. I couldn't believe my eyes, it was the same gal I saw on Old Miller Road a couple days before.

"Daddy, I saw that gal a couple days ago walking down Old Miller Road!"

"You sho boy?"

"Yes sa."

"Who was she with?"

"She wasn't with nobody she was walking by her self, she said hey and I said hey. What happened to her daddy?"

"I don't know fo sho boy, and I don't know if we'll ever know!"

We dropped Billy Ray off down by the road near his house and we rode into town to get the sheriff. The sheriff didn't seem real concerned when my daddy told him it was a colored gal, he just said "I'll get there when I can." My daddy's old mule pulled that wagon back to the river before the sheriff and old doc Smith got there in his truck, and that old mule is blind in one eye and he's as old as dirt. We never found out who she was, where she came from or what happened. Sheriff Banks said she was just a colored gal, that's all.

Chapter 3

Midnight

Billy Ray and I didn't see much of each other during the school year because colored children and white children went to different schools. Billy Ray's school was on the other side of Burdonville and it was painted bright red and they had a real teacher. Not that anything was wrong with the way Reverend Hightower taught us because I think he did a good job, it's just that he was a Reverend and not a school teacher. The following summer started like any other summer. Reverend Hightower rang the church bell and all the colored children headed for the fields to work with their families. And as usual, I grabbed my fishing pole and headed for the river. Shortly after I got to the river, Billy Ray showed up. While we were at the river fishing, we talked about making a tree house out of an old shack across the river. Then out of the clear blue sky Billy Ray asked me the strangest question.

"Hey Jeremiah, what it feel like to be colored?"

"What?" I said.

"What it feel like to be colored?"

"...I don't know, I suppose good sometimes, and bad other times."

"What do da good feel like Jeremiah?"

"Well, white folks talking bout da depression and hard times and such."

"Why does dat feel good Jeremiah?"

"Cause colored folk always got hard times, now white folk know how it feels."

"What do da bad feel like?"

"White folks calling us names, like nigger, dog, dirty coon and such."

"Yep, I suppose dat do feel bad," said Billy Ray.

"What it feel like to be white Billy Ray?" I asked.

"Well, I can be the President of the United States, dat job is fo white men only," Billy Ray said with pride.

"Why?" I asked.

"Cause dat's da way thangs is," he said.

"But how come jest white men always get to be president?"

"I don't know, I suppose dat's da way da good Lord wanted it," he said.

"Do you thank da good Lord loves colored folk da same as white folk?"

"I reckon so, I don't know to much bout da good Lord," he said.

We sat there quietly for the rest of the afternoon, I suppose we were both thinking about what the other had said. We never did catch any fish that day, I reckon we scared off all the fish talking and carrying on. Later that afternoon Billy Ray started talking about cowboys and Indians and such.

"I saw a horse jest running free in a pasture and it don't belong to nobody, and if we could catch em, we could be real cowboys, Jeremiah."

"How you know it don't belong to nobody, Billy Ray?"

"Cause it don't live in no barn or stables or nothing, he's jest running free."

"But what if he do belong to somebody, and dey catch us riding him?"

"I'm telling you Jeremiah, he don't belong to nobody."

"But if he do, dat be horse stealing, and dey hang you for dat."

"Ain't nobody gonna get hung, now come on Jeremiah and stop being a scary cat."

"Stop calling me a scary cat Billy Ray, I ain't scared, I jest don't want my daddy to find out dat's all! Don't choo ever think about what choo doin befoe you do it Billy Ray?"

"I think you think to much. Why you always worrying bout yo daddy anyway?"

"Cause my daddy will beat me good if'in I get into some more trouble."

"I promise, nuttin's gonna happen. You got my word on it!"

At that moment I heard that soft voice again telling me, *"don't go."* But I didn't want to miss out on riding a real wild horse, so I ignored the voice.

",,,,,,,,,Well,,,,,alright den."

We left our fishing poles right there at the river and headed off to find the horse Billy Ray saw in some pasture. We walked past several work farms and saw lots of colored field hands and white field hands working side by side in the scorching sun. They looked tired and worn out, and some of the women folk had babies tied to their backs like a bundle of cotton. The colored folks were singing like they were in church, and I could hear the steady rhythm of that old mule stomping along the ground holding the drum beat, and the plow scratching the dirt sounds like old shoes sliding on a wooden floor.

Along the way we found a ear of corn on the side of the road, it must have fell off someone's wagon on the way to the market. We picked it up to feed the horse if we ever found him. According to Billy Ray's pocket watch, we must have walked for two hours before we found that horse.

He was a beautiful black stallion with a long shiny mane and tail. He walked with his head held high as he pranced toward us, like he didn't have no fear at all. That horse walked right up to me and Billy Ray like he knew us. We gave him some corn and he ate it right out of our hands.

"I told choo we'd find em Jeremiah."

"A horse dis fine got to belong to somebody," I said.

"If'n you owned a horse like dis, would you jest leave em way out here in da field with nobody to tend to em?" asked Billy Ray.

"Well, maybe not, but dis ain't my horse neither," I said.

"Lets take em for a ride, Jeremiah."

"I don't think that's such a good idea, Billy Ray."

"Ah, come on, stop being a scary cat."

"I done told choo, I ain't no scary cat, I jest don't think dis such a good idea."

"Well, I ain't scared, and I ain't walking all da way back home," he said.

I kept hearing that soft voice telling me, *"don't do it, you know better."*

",,,,,,,well,,,well,,,,,alright," I said reluctantly.

"Now you talking Jeremiah, come on, help me get on den I'll pull ya up."

Billy Ray climbed up on that black stallion like it was his very own horse, then he helped me get on. We didn't have no reins or nothing, so Billy Ray just pulled his mane to make him go left or right. We gave him a little kick and he took off running. I was holding on to Billy Ray with all my might, after a while that black stallion started walking real easy like.

"We need to give em a name, don't choo think so Jeremiah?"

"Yea, what about, Blacky?" I said.

"Naw, that sounds like a dogs name, what bout "Midnight" cause he's as black as night?"

"Dat sounds good," I said.

"Then Midnight it is, giddy up Midnight we got to get home fo it gets dark."

On the way home we went right back past those field hands, only this time they were leaving the fields and going home. I remember seeing some youngins just like me and Billy Ray walking with the field hands. As we rode by they were staring at us like something was wrong. One of the older colored men stopped us.

"Where bouts you youngins get dis here horse?" he asked.

"We found em running free in da fields up yonder," said Billy Ray.

Those field hands looked at one another and started to shake their heads.

"Ya'll youngins betta take dis horse back where you got em from, fo Mr. Taylor come lookin for dis prize stallion."

"Who's Mr. Taylor?" I asked.

"He's dat white man dat own all dis here land and dat horse ya'll sittin on boy, and I know fo a fact dat Mr. Taylor don't like nobody stealing from em, let alone a little colored boy," he said.

"Well I ain't colored," Billy Ray yelled.

"Dat may be true, but, if'n Mr. Taylor catch you youngins on dis horse, it ain't gonna make no never mind to him what color you is, he'll whip da life out choo too."

At that point the field hands started walking away, while me and Billy Ray just sat there. I was scared and didn't know what to do, so I decided to get off Midnight and start walking home. Billy Ray was angry, he acted like that horse really did belong to him. Billy Ray rode that horse along side as I walked.

"I ain't scared Jeremiah, we found dis horse running free and we caught em."

"Billy Ray, dat horse wasn't running free, he was in a field dat belong to Mr. Taylor, dat means he belongs to Mr. Taylor," I said.

"Well, I ain't taking em back, maybe we can ride em da rest of da way home, den let em go and he'll find his way back home," said Billy Ray.

"Maybe."

"What choo mean maybe?"

"Maybe, maybe he will and maybe he won't. Ain't no telling what a horse gonna do," I said.

"Dat's true. Well, let's jest ride em da rest of da way home and see."

"Naw, dat ain't such a good idea Billy Ray, we should jest take em back right now."

"Dat's to far to go back, and if I get home to late my daddy will skin me alive, now you don't want me to get a lickin do ya?"

"Well, alright, but as soon as we get home we gonna turn em loose and send em home," I proclaimed.

"Alright den, get back up here." Billy Ray demanded.

I climbed back on Midnight and we headed home, pretending to be real cowboys as we rode into the sunset. As soon as we got to Billy Ray's house, he jumped off Midnight and ran toward his house.

"See ya tomorrow Jeremiah."

"See ya tomorrow Billy Ray."

I rode Midnight toward my house by myself and as I rode I heard that soft voice again telling me to, *"get off and just let him go back."* But I was having to much fun riding him, so I just ignored the soft voice.

Shortly after I left Billy Ray I heard a truck coming up behind me. My heart started to race, I just knew I was in big trouble, so I jumped off Midnight and ran into the woods to hide, but Midnight followed me and that truck followed Midnight. I thought I found a good hiding place down by the river in a cave but Midnight was standing right out front drinking water out of the river. Suddenly I heard a loud voice coming from the woods.

"Come out of there boy, I know your in there," the man yelled.

I was to afraid to move so I just sat there quiet as a mouse, but that man didn't go away.

"Now if you don't come out of there I'm gonna let my dog loose and he's gonna come in there and fetch you out," he yelled.

Well, I didn't want to come out of that cave, but at the same time I didn't want to stay there either. That dog started barking and growling as if I were a raccoon. I could almost feel his breath on my hand as I pushed back up against that cave wall. That dog wasn't about to let me go so I decided to come on out. Mr. Taylor was so mad I thought he was going to hang me for sure. He grabbed me by my collar and dragged me out of that cave while that old dog of his was trying to take a bite out of me. He managed to hold that dog back, but barely. I was so scared I do believe I stopped breathing once or twice, and my heart was pounding so fast it felt like it was gonna burst right out of my chest.

"You little horse thief, I ought a string yo little narrow black ass up to dat tree over yonda!"

"Please sa, please, I ain't no thief, I was gonna turn em loose and send em home," I cried.

"You look like a thief to me boy, do you know how much dat horse cost?"

"No sa, no sa,,,, we didn't hurt em none sa, we was jest riding em dats all."

"We, who's we boy, I don't see nobody but choo?" he said.

I remember thinking for a moment that I didn't want to tell on Billy Ray. But at the same time, I didn't want to get into trouble by myself either. All I could think about was Mr. Taylor whipping the life out of me, like that colored field hand said. He didn't look like the kind of white man that would tolerate lies so I just told him I was alone. He didn't waste no time talking after that. He pulled out his horse whip and whipped me but good. He whipped me so bad my clothes just fell off my body into rags. He left me right there by the river, and somehow, I managed to make my way home in the dark.

When I got home my momma cleaned me up. She mixed up some ashes and grease then put it on my wounds, it hurt like heck but it kept me from getting an infection. I'll never forget the look on my daddy's face when he saw me all beat and whipped. When he spoke that little old house rumbled and shook like it was gonna fall down. I can still hear him hollering to this day.

"Who did dis to ya boy?" he yelled. "Now don't choo lie to me."

I couldn't tell my daddy the truth, because I knew he'd go over to Mr. Taylor's farm and kill him for what he did to me. If he did that the white folks in town would have burned down our little house and killed all of us, and I couldn't let that happen.

"I don't know daddy, I was jest fishin down by da river, and somebody started whuppin me."

"Who was it?" he asked.

"I don't know daddy, I was to scared to look."

"Was he white, colored, or what boy?" he demanded to know.

"I don't know daddy, I couldn't see his face."

"I'm goin down to dat river, and if I catch da man dat did dis, I'll kill em dead. All yall big boys come wit me," he said.

My daddy and older brothers took their shot guns and went down to the river. I remember hoping and praying that Mr. Taylor was long gone with that horse of his, because if he wasn't, he would have died for sure that night.

I stayed awake all night waiting for my daddy to come home.

"Please Lord, let my daddy and brothers come home safe, and don't let dem hurt Mr. Taylor," I prayed.

Late that night my daddy and brothers came home and I could hear my daddy telling my momma that they couldn't find nothing or nobody near that river. I was so relieved cause nobody got killed, especially my daddy and brothers. The next day Billy Ray came looking for me and my momma told him I couldn't come out for a couple of days because I wasn't feeling well. She didn't tell him what happened because she knew it could mean trouble if white folk started asking questions and such. Somehow I think my momma always knew Billy Ray had something to do with that whuppin I took, but she never let on and I never told Billy Ray.

Chapter 4

God's Creatures

Several weeks have passed and I decided to go fishing. I went down to the river on a hot humid morning and on my way I heard a noise on the other side of some bushes. I slowly crept up to the bushes and peaked through to see what I could see. To my surprise, it was Billy Ray, and he had a jack rabbit caught in a snare. He was throwing rocks at it while it was squirming and fighting for it's life. Billy Ray just stared at that rabbit and laughed. I heard that soft voice say, *"stop him,"* so I jumped out of the bushes and said,

"What choo doing to dat rabbit Billy Ray?"

"Hey Jeremiah, I ain't seen you in a month a Sundays, where you been hiding?"

"I ain't been hiding Billy Ray, I jest been doing chores round da farm."

"Seems like you been hide'n to me."

"Naw, I jest been busy dats all. What choo doin to dat rabbit?"

"I was jest seein how long it take for em to die."

"What choo doin dat fo Billy Ray?"

"I don't know, I jest like doin it, dats all."

"Dat rabbit ain't done nothin to nobody," I said. "Why don't choo let em go?"

"What choo makin such a fuss about Jeremiah, it's jest a stupid old rabbit?"

"Yea, but how'd you like it if somebody tie you up and chunk rocks at choo?"

"I suppose dat wouldn't be much fun," said Billy Ray. "I'll let em go!"

Billy Ray untied that rabbit and it took off running into the woods as fast it could. Billy Ray had a strange look on his face, he seemed to be angry about letting that rabbit go but he just smiled. When we started to walk down toward the river I saw three or four dead rabbits, a couple of squirrels and one or two birds. They were all covered with blood and I could tell that they had been hit with rocks because of the way the fur was ripped off and the feathers were all ruffled. When we got down to the river I asked Billy Ray how long had he been killing small animals and such and he said,

"If'n I find the right kinda rock, I can hit a bird while it's flying."

"Why you kill all dem rabbits, squirrels and birds Billy Ray, if you ain't gonna take em home fo supper," I asked. "And why you smile when you do it?"

"I don't know, don't nobody care, dey jest some dumb animals ain't dey?"

"Dem animals is God's creatures, and I don't think He'd take kindly to you killing em fo no reason at all, Billy Ray."

"What about choo Jeremiah, you be killing fish all da time?"

"Yea, but I takes em home for supper, I don't leave em on da ground to die."

"You ain't no different dan me Jeremiah, you like killing dem stupid animals jest like I do."

"Naw, you wrong, I don't like doing no such thang."

"You mean to tell me you don't be having fun when you fishing?"

"It be fun, but not da kinda fun you talkin bout."

"What kinda fun you talkin bout Jeremiah?"

"Well, I knows my momma and daddy gonna be happy when I bring home some catfish or rabbit fo supper," I said. "Dats da kinda fun I'm talkin bout."

"My daddy buys fresh meat from da country store in town, so I don't have to fish and hunt fo supper Jeremiah."

"Well, my family ain't got dat kinda money to do dat, so we makes do wit what we have round here," I said. "Besides, dem animals you killed ain't gonna serve no purpose jest layin under dem bushes."

"Why don't choo take em home Jeremiah, maybe yo momma can cook em up."

"Naw, I don't thank dat would be a good idea, Billy Ray."

"Why not, you said dem animals ain't gonna serve no purpose jest layin under dem bushes!"

"Yea, but dem animals been suffering and rotting in da sun, dey need to be buried."

"You mean like a funeral, wit words said over em and such," he asked.

"I suppose so, after all dey is God's creatures," I said.

Billy Ray never did seem to understand that what he did was wrong. We buried all those animals that morning and said a few Christian words over them. I often wondered how many other animals Billy Ray killed for the fun of it. He seemed to do it with such ease, without any remorse or after thought. The strange thing was, Billy Ray had the ability to make me laugh one moment then scare the mess out of me the next.

I don't know if I ever thought of Billy Ray Horton as my best friend after that, but I sure thought of him as someone to keep an eye on! We remained friends over the next few years and it seemed as though Billy Ray was always coming up with some crazy scheme that would get me in trouble. I didn't hear that soft voice for a while, and I often wondered where it came from and how come it was always warning me when something bad was about to happen. I didn't tell Billy Ray about the voices I heard for a while, I suppose I didn't want him to think I was going crazy and such, so I kept it to myself.

Chapter 5

The Angel Appears

From the first time I met Billy Ray Horton it seemed as though something bad was always happening. On my fourteenth birthday my momma baked me a chocolate cake and all my brothers and sisters gathered around the table and sang happy birthday to me. My daddy didn't do much singing, he just stood there and smiled. He handed me a present wrapped in some cloth and when I opened it I was happy to see it was a book. He knew I loved to read. Daddy didn't believe in wasting time but momma would always talk him into coming in early from the fields when ever one of us had a birthday.

When momma wasn't working she would spend countless hours reading her bible and praying. On Sunday morning momma made sure we all were clean and polished for Sunday morning church service. Momma used to wear that same yellow dress every Sunday, as a matter of fact, momma wore that same dress to funerals, weddings, and social functions too. It didn't matter to her that it was her only good dress she always had her head held high. She would always tell us that she was about the Lords business so as long as your clothes were clean it didn't matter what you wore.

Momma loved going to church and talking with the women folk afterwards and that was the only day daddy wasn't working in the fields, because momma used to tell him, that even the good Lord rested on the seventh day. I remember those Sunday morning church services like it was yesterday, all the colored folk in New Bethlehem would gather to hear Reverend Hightower preach. He never went past the six grade himself but he was a good teacher and a preacher.

He was always happy and he used to sing and preach at the same time. Momma and all the other folk sure did seem to enjoy listening to him. They would say "amen" every time he said something, and "praise the Lord" after he finished singing. Now I don't no to much about preachers but Reverend Hightower and that choir was the best I'd ever seen. One song I clearly remember the choir and the Reverend singing was, "I know it was the blood." I can still hear them singing,

"I know it was the blood of Jesus,
I know it was the blood of Jesus,
I know it was the blood of Jesus for me.
One day when I was lost, He died upon the cross.
And I know it was the blood for me.
They pierced Him in His side,
They pierced Him in His side,
They pierced Him in His side for me.
One day when I was lost, He died upon the cross.
And I know it was the blood for me.
His blood came streaming down,
His blood came streaming down,
His blood came streaming down for me.
One day when I was lost, He died upon the cross.
And I know it was the blood for me."

After the choir finished singing Reverend Hightower slowly walked up to the pulpit and in a powerful voice he would say, "I know it was the blood." Then the congregation would say "Amen." "They pierced Him in his side, and His blood came streaming down," he said. Then the congregation would all say "Amen, preach Reverend." Reverend Hightower would always start his sermons with the same prayer! "Father God we give you all the honor, power and glory this morning. We ask for your blessing upon this church and all your sheep who have gathered here in this place to hear your holy word. We thank you father God that each and every person under the sound of my voice is walking in divine health, and we thank you that all of our fields will yield an abundance of cotton, fruits and vegetables.

Thank you Father for all that you've done and all that you will do, in Jesus name I pray, amen. And all the saints said…Amen." Reverend Hightower used to carry a big black bible that was worn and torn, and he could flip to any verse anytime anywhere somebody had a question. "Turn with me if you will to Genesis Chapter four, verse one through nine,

Verse one, *And Adam knew his wife; and she conceived, and bare Cain, and she said, I have gotten a man from the cord.*

Verse two, *And she again bare his brother Abel, and Abel was a keeper of sheep, but Cain was a tiller of the ground.*

Verse three, *And in the process of time it came to pass, that Cain brought of the fruit of the ground and offering unto the Lord.*

Verse four, *And Abel, he also brought of his firstlings of his flock and of the fat thereof. And the Lord had respect unto Abel and to his offering.*

Verse five, *But unto Cain and to his offering He had no respect. And Cain was very wroth, and his countenance fell.*

Verse six, *And the Lord said unto Cain, why art thou wroth? And why is thy countenance fallen?*

Verse seven, *If thou doest well, shalt thou not be accepted? And if thou doest not well, sin lieth at the door. And unto thee shall be his desire, and thou shalt rule over him.*

Verse eight, *And Cain talked with Abel his brother: And it came to pass, when they were in the field, that Cain rose up against Abel his brother, and slew him.*

Verse nine, *And the Lord said unto Cain, where is Abel thy brother? And he said, I know not: Am I my brother's keeper?*

The entire congregation said "Amen, preach Reverend, preach." Then Reverend Hightower said, "Absolutely, is God's answer. Not only are we our brother's keeper, we are held accountable for our treatment of and our ways of relating to our brothers, both blood and spiritual." I'll never forget that sermon as long as I live because it was at that point in my life that I began to understand who I was. I accepted Jesus Christ as my Lord and Savior that Sunday and after church the whole congregation sang "Wade in the water" as we walked down to the river. When we got down to the river, Reverend Hightower and I waded in. He placed his hand over my forehead and asked me,

"Do you Jeremiah Liggons believe that Jesus Christ is the son of God, and that He gave his only son to die on a cross for your sins that you might have the right to the tree of life?"

"Yessa, I do," I said.

"Then I baptize you in the name of the Father, the Son and the Holy Ghost."

Then he dipped me under the water with his massive hands, and when I came up I coughed and tried to clear my throat as everyone clapped their hands and smiled at me. As we started to get out of the water I saw a bright light glowing over the river, I didn't know what it was at the time, but I was sure nobody else saw it but me. Then It slowly disappeared as suddenly as it came.

I felt strange inside, I didn't know how I was supposed to feel but I did know I was different. After I got baptized everybody was shaken my hands and hugging me, I felt like I was important not just a little nappy headed boy anymore. While I was walking through the crowd getting my hands shaked and congratulated and such, I saw Billy Ray peeking around the corner of the church. He was barefooted as usual and he was eating a green apple. I know where that green apple came from and I sure didn't want any part of it. I went over to Billy Ray and asked, "Did you see me get baptized?"

"Yep, I sho did, what choo feel like now Jeremiah?"

"I don't rightly no, kinda tingly inside, like I got butter flies in my tummy."

"You look da same Jeremiah."

"I don't think I'm supposed to look different, ain't choo ever been baptized?"

"Naw, I ain't never been baptized, my momma and daddy don't go to church and such. My daddy say church is for colored folk and women."

"I ain't never heard dat kinda talk Billy Ray."

"Well, my daddy talk like dat all da time."

"My momma say, folk dat don't love Jesus gonna go to hell when dey die."

"What do you think it's like in hell Jeremiah?"

"Momma say it be a thousand times worse than being a colored man in da south," I said.

"Sho nuff?"

"Yep, and you know how bad colored folk got it round here," I said.

"Yep, dats pretty bad alright," said Billy Ray

We stood there on the side of that old church for a while, neither one of us had to much to say after that. Billy Ray had a strange look on his face as if he were worried about something or someone. Looking back in retrospect he was probably thinking about his own fate and mortality, who knows, he never did say what was on his mind. After a while all the church folk started leaving, most of them were walking but some had horses and buck boards to ride and a few had cars.

"Come on home Jeremiah," momma said.

"I'll be there directly, momma."

"Do you have to go right now Jeremiah?"

"Yep, momma gonna fix a chicken celebration dinner," I said with excitement. "Dat sounds good Jeremiah, but let me sho you somethin fo you go."

Billy Ray reached in his pocket and pulled out a pack of cigarettes.

"What's dat Billy Ray?"

"You sho is ignorant Jeremiah, ain't choo ever seen a pack a cigarettes befoe?"

"Naw, I ain't never seen em in no pack befoe, where'd dey come from?"

"I got em out my daddy's drawer."

"Ain't he gonna get mad at choo, Billy Ray?"

"He's got allot of em ever since he took over my uncles farm."

"Is yo daddy rich now Billy Ray?"

"I don't rightly know if he's rich, but he always seem to have money now."

"What choo gonna do wit dem cigarettes Billy Ray?"

"I'm gonna smoke em, what choo thank, don't choo wanna try one?" he asked.

"Naw, not me."

"Scary cat, scary cat, Jeremiah's a scary cat."

I was tired of Billy Ray always calling me a scary cat, simply because I didn't want to do something, but I didn't want to look like one neither. But suddenly and out of nowhere that bright light I saw down by the river appeared just a couple of feet behind Billy Ray.

"What's wrong Jeremiah, you look like you done seen a ghost or somethin?"

I tried to ignore the bright light and show Billy Ray I wasn't scared even though I was.

"I done told choo I ain't no scary cat. Gimmie one a dem cigarettes Billy Ray."

I took a cigarette from Billy Ray and put it in my mouth. Then Billy Ray struck a match on the side of the old church and lit my cigarette. I started coughing and choking so bad I thought I was going to die and as usual Billy Ray started laughing and rolling on the ground.

He thought that was the funniest thing he had ever seen. He must of laughed five or ten minutes. After I stopped coughing I had a real bad burning sensation in my chest and throat. It felt like my insides were on fire. Billy Ray finally stopped laughing and said,

"Let me show you how to do it Jeremiah," he said as he struck a match and lit the cigarette.

As Billy Ray inhaled the smoke he started coughing and choking just as bad as I did, now it was my turn to laugh at him. He coughed so hard he started vomiting all over the place. After he stopped coughing we both realized that cigarettes weren't very fun so we just threw them away and went down to the river. While we were down at the river we talked about my baptism.

"Now dat choo baptized Jeremiah, are you gonna start preachin and such?"

"Naw, I ain't no preacher, I jest accepted Jesus Christ as my Lord and Savior."

"What's da Lord gonna save you from?"

"You know, sins and such. Jesus died on da cross fo all my sins."

"What did he go and do dat fo Jeremiah?"

"My momma say cause God loved da world so much, dat he gave His only son."

"I don't think I'd give my only son, what about choo Jeremiah?"

"Well, I ain't God, but He sho must a love dis old world to let em kill His son."

"I suppose dat was a whole lot a love, huh, Jeremiah?"

"Sho was."

While we sat on those muddy banks we started to smell something burning.

"You smell dat Billy Ray?"

"Yep, smell like smoke."

At that moment we turned around and to our surprise the church was on fire. The flames were as high as the bell in the tower. We quickly got up and started running for help.

"Fire, fire, fire, da old church on fire," I yelled.

The colored folk in the area must have already smelled the smoke or seen the flames because they were already running toward the church with buckets. The men folk ran straight to the river and started passing buckets of water to one another and tossing it into the flames. That fire was so big and strong, not one bucket of water made a difference. That old church burned to the ground and all the men folk could do was stand back and watch. The women folk fell to their knees and started crying and praying. After the smoke died down, the men folk started asking questions, they were very angry and thought that white folks had something to do with the old church burning down.

"We cain't have nothin, seems like white folk bent on drivin us out," said Mr. Brown.

"White folk been trying to burn us out ever since slavery ended," said Mr. Johnson. "Now da chiren ain't got no school, and we ain't got no church."

"Well, I don't know bout choo all, but I ain't gonna stand back and do nothin," said Mr. Washington

"What do you suggest we do Mr. Washington, go round burning white churches and schools?" said Reverend Hightower.

"Naw, dat ain't what I'm saying Reverend."

"We don't know for sure who set dis here fire, and we sho don't know if white folks is responsible," said Reverend Hightower.

"Then what do you suggest we do Reverend?"

"Everybody go home, I'll go to town and talk to sheriff Banks."

"Da sheriff? Dat old sheriff ain't gonna do nothin Reverend, he jest as well burn dat old church his self."

"Don't talk like that brother Washington, talk like that can get you lynched."

"Maybe so Reverend, but at least I'm talkin what be true."

As it started to get late all the men folk continued to argue about what to do while the women folk stayed on their knees praying. I remember watching my momma cry and pray for what seemed like hours. I started day dreaming and thinking about my ancestors. They tell me that my great granddaddy helped build that old church after slavery, and the graveyard out back had graves dating back to the early 1800's. When I stood near the graveyard, I couldn't help but think of all the history that land holds. In that graveyard behind that old church is buried slaves, former slaves, service men, house wives, children and free men.

The stories they'd tell would fill a library. The knowledge and wisdom that is buried there is overwhelming. That's why we must honor and respect our elders while their with us, because what they have to offer can't be found in any books. They could teach us things about being colored Americans that we've never thought of. Sometimes I try to imagine what it must have been like to work seemingly endless hours from sun up until sundown in the blazing heat and freezing snow, with no pay, no gratitude, very little clothing or shelter, and with death the only guarantee of freedom. Where pain and suffering are constant companions, and to be bread like cattle and sold much the same. Whipped, beaten, raped, lynched and murdered, the only comforts were old Negro spirituals, beautiful songs of prayer and praise with hidden messages of hope and whispers of freedom.

I often imagine what it must have been like to live in a land that my people walked for thousands of years, and where the air was fresh and the water was pure. I imagine an open air classroom where every day and night was a lesson of education and survival and living among nature and dwelling in its riches and glory. To study plants and animals that one day might save a life and calculate the stars in the firmament. Where generation after generation, pride, dignity, loyalty, and honor are passed down like a golden baton, precise and oh so accurate! I remember standing there day dreaming about the past, when suddenly I heard the voice of Annie Mae. Annie Mae was a sixteen year old colored gal with a big mouth. She was fare skinned and skinny and she was always getting into someone else's business, gossiping and such. She walked right up to the men folk and said,

"It wasn't no white folks dat burned down da church."

Reverend Hightower looked stunned, and all the men folk stopped arguing for a moment to listen to Annie Mae.

"What choo talkin bout gal?" said Mr. Washington.

"I said, it wasn't no white folks dat burned down da church."

"Annie Mae, if you know something, you best tell it," said Reverend Hightower.

"Well, after Jeremiah got baptized, I stayed behind to pick wild flowers fo my momma, and I seen it."

"Speak up gal, what choo see?" said Mr. Johnson.

"I seen Billy Ray Horton and Jeremiah smokin cigarettes on the side of the church."

At that moment I was stunned. I couldn't believe Annie Mae thought we started the fire. I thought she must have been crazy or something, I knew we didn't start that fire but we were smoking cigarettes.

My daddy was furious, he came over to where I was standing and snatched me off the ground.

"Is dat true boy?" he yelled.

I knew I couldn't tell a lie but I was to afraid to tell the truth and as usual Billy Ray was long gone. My daddy started shaking me like a rag doll.

"I'm talkin to you boy, was you smokin cigarettes by da church?"

I paused for a moment then reluctantly answered even though I knew I was going to get a whuppin.

"Yes sa, I, I, I, was smokin, but I didn't start no fire daddy, I jest took one puff and started coughin and chokin, den I threw dat old cigarette on da ground."

At that moment I knew what must have happened. When we threw those cigarettes into the dry grass they must have caught on fire and burned the church. But it was to late for excuses and my daddy and the rest of the men were very angry.

"Why was you smokin in da first place Jeremiah, you jest got baptized?"

"I don't know daddy, I jest tried it one time."

"Where'd you get some cigarettes anyway, dat Billy Ray Horton I bet?"

"No sa, I found em on da road."

My daddy pulled off his leather belt and started whuppin me like there was no tomorrow. That whuppin felt like it lasted an hour. All the church folk stood and watched, including Annie Mae. She had a funny little smile on her face like she enjoyed watching folk in pain. I remember looking out of the corner of my eye and seeing Billy Ray watching from around a pine tree.

He had tears in his eyes but that didn't compare to the tears I had. After that whuppin my momma and daddy took me home and told me to stay away from Billy Ray Horton. "I don't ever want to see you round Billy Ray Horton no mo, dat boy ain't nothin but trouble, you hear me Jeremiah?" he said.

"Yes sa, but he's my friend daddy."

"Jeremiah, don't let me tell you again, stay away from dat boy."

"Yes sa."

"Now carry yo narrow butt to bed, fo I get mad again," he yelled.

"Yes daddy."

I went to bed that night with no supper and no extra slice of my birthday cake but that was the least of my concerns, what I really wanted was for my momma to know I didn't mean to set that old church on fire. Late that night I could hear my daddy snoring in the other room and the sound of his rocking chair squeaking out on the porch. I knew it had to be momma because any time she was upset about something she'd rock in daddy's old rocking chair late at night. So

I got out of bed and snuck around the back of the house and came up on the side of the porch. I knew I couldn't let daddy catch me or I'd get another whuppin so I was as quiet as a church mouse. When I got around to the side of the porch I could see momma's face. She looked as though she had seen a ghost and she was crying. She was slowly rocking back and forth with her bible on her lap and she was still wearing her special yellow dress, and black patent leather shoes. She wasn't praying, just staring into the night sky.

"Momma," I said with a whisper.

She didn't look down at me but I knew she heard me, she just kept staring into the night sky as if she were waiting for something to fall.

"I'm sorry momma, I didn't mean fo dis to happen, I'm real sorry."

"I know your sorry Jeremiah, but what choo did was wrong son, and you need to be on your knees right now askin da good Lord for forgiveness."

I remember falling to my knees as fast as I could, I put my hands together and closed my eyes as tight as I could and started to pray.

"Dear Lord, it's me, Jeremiah. I'm sorry fo burning down yo house, I didn't do it on purpose, it was a accident. Please forgive me Lord, and don't send me to hell, I promise I'll be good from now on. I'll work in dem fields wit daddy all day even though he say I'm to scrawny. I'll tote water, clean up after da chickens and da hogs. I'll catch a bunch a fish and give em to the church folk, jest so dey know I'm sorry fo what I did. Please Lord, don't send me to hell, I'm sorry. In Jesus name I pray, Amen."

"Jeremiah, the good Lord ain't gonna send you to hell."

"But I burned down da church momma, you said dats God's house."

"Yes you did, but the good Lord loves you anyway, He knows your heart son and He's already forgiven you," she said.

A huge burden had been lifted from my shoulders that night and I felt as though everything was going to be alright. I went back to bed and went to sleep. The next morning I got up early and got ready with my daddy, brothers and sisters to go work in the field. My oldest brother Abraham saw me getting ready and asked,

"Where you thank you goin, bones?"

"Quit calling me bones, my name be Jeremiah, and I'm goin to work wit ya'll."

They all started laughing and making fun of me. I didn't appreciate it and neither did my daddy and he let them know it.

"Ya'll stop all dis carryin on, and stop makin fun of yo brother. Jeremiah, I knows you want to make up fo what choo did yesterday, but what I need fo you to do is take care of thangs round here."

"But daddy, I promised da Lord I'd work wit ya'll to help out and such."

"Da Lord understand you mean well but I want you round here tendin da chickens, hogs and fishin and such, you hear me boy?" he said. "Yes sa."

I was very disappointed but I didn't have much choice in the matter. My family left the house before sun up and headed to the fields. Momma put on her work clothes and went to town to work in Mrs. Peterson's house. I stood still for a moment looking around the house as if I didn't know what to do next. The silence was eerie, unlike I had ever noticed before. I didn't hear the chickens out in the yard, or the hogs in the pen, and I couldn't even hear my family singing on their way to the fields. Suddenly, that bright light appeared just as it had the last time I saw it down by the river the day before. But this time it was different. It had sparkles that look like fire flies flying all around it. As I stared at it I couldn't move, it was the most beautiful sight I had ever seen.

As I stared at it it slowly began to take shape, and within the light I could see wings, beautiful huge white wings. Then a face appeared, it was a face unlike any I had ever seen before in my life. It was a face of a woman. She wasn't colored, and she wasn't white, she was just light, and she was beautiful. She was wearing a long white robe and she had long flowing black hair that seemed to blow in the wind even though we were inside. I was amazed and unable to move, I just stared at her without blinking. She reached out and touched me but I didn't feel a thing, but I know she was touching my hand because I could see her hand on mine. She spoke without moving her mouth.

"God knows your heart Jeremiah and He has a wonderful plan for your life. Study the bible and never doubt His word and He'll always take care of you."

Oh dear God I thought, the soft voice, and just like that she disappeared.

Chapter 6

Friendly Relations

A little over two years had passed and I was now sixteen, I didn't see much of Billy Ray but we would run into each other from time to time in town or down at the river when I was fishing. He started hanging around some white boys from the other side of town. Their families were wealthy and I suppose Billy Ray wanted to fit in with them, especially since his daddy acted like he was rich and such. His daddy was always having parties and inviting all the rich white folk over to his plantation house. That summer I snuck over to Billy Ray's house to see what all the fuss was about. I saw white men with the finest clothes on walking with canes even though there wasn't anything wrong with their legs. I saw white women with umbrellas, and there wasn't a cloud in the sky, as a matter of fact, it was a warm summer evening.

They were talking in small groups all over the yard and in the house, and I remember a band playing music while some white folks were dancing. I moved in to get a closer look, and low and behold I saw Billy Ray, he was dressed in a fine black suit. Billy Ray was talking to Peggy Lynn Peterson, my momma used to clean her house and cook her meals until Mrs. Peterson took sick and died. Momma said Mrs. Peterson drank to much corn liquor and just drank herself to death, but white folk say she only drank to ease her pain.

I don't know what pain white folks had but it can't be worse than what colored folk had. I must have watched Billy Ray and Peggy Lynn for hours, they looked as though they were having a fine time. After a while Billy Ray and Peggy Lynn went for a walk into the woods, I couldn't imagine why they would leave such a fine party and what they were going into the woods for, so I followed. They were holding hands and such then they started kissing. Billy Ray was trying to take Peggy Lynn's dress off but she wouldn't let him but he just kept begging and pulling her clothes until she slapped his face.

"Stop it Billy Ray," she yelled.

"What's wrong Peggy Lynn, why are you teasing?" he asked. "I know you want to do it."

"I most certainly do not," she said with the accent of a southern belle.

"Ahhh, come on Peggy Lynn, nobody's gonna know, it'll be our little secret."

Peggy Lynn got real mad and started walking back to the party. Billy Ray grabbed her arm and tried to apologize.

"Peggy Lynn wait, I'm sorry, I didn't mean it," he said.

"Don't you ever talk to me like that again Billy Ray Horton, I'm not some little colored gal, I'm a southern lady, don't you ever forget that," she said.

"I won't Peggy Lynn, I promise."

Billy Ray and Peggy Lynn held hands and walked back to the party. When they got back to the party everyone was starting to leave. I watched as the last car drove away. When I started to leave I saw Billy Ray sneak out the side door and run into the woods toward New Bethlehem. I followed Billy Ray until he stopped near a small house. When I tried to get closer I stepped on a branch and made so much noise Billy Ray heard me and turned around and caught me watching him.

"Jeremiah, is dat choo?"

"Yea Billy Ray it be me."

"What choo doin out here, Jeremiah?"

"What choo doin out here, Billy Ray?"

"I was, ahhh,,,I was jest passin bye and I heard a strange noise, so I stopped to check it out, what about choo Jeremiah, what choo doing out here?"

"I was ahh,,, ahhh,, I was followin you Billy Ray."

"Followin me, what choo mean followin me?"

"I followed you from yo daddy's party."

"You was at da party?"

"Yep,,,well,, I was in da woods watchin."

"Why didn't you come up to da house?" he asked.

"I don't think all dem fancy white folk would of been to happy to see me."

"Ahh, dats nonsense Jeremiah, daddy wouldn't mind you comin over."

"Maybe not yo daddy, but da rest of dem white folk might not be so friendly."

"Yea, I suppose your right Jeremiah," he said. "You want to see somethin special, Jeremiah?"

"Sho! What?"

"You'll see, come on."

We continued to walk toward the little house and as it turns out it was Sara James's house on the out skirts of town. Sara was a colored girl about sixteen or seventeen years old. She lived in that little house with her momma and three sisters. She was fare skinned and pretty and all the colored boys in town were chasing after her but she was always acting high and mighty. When Billy Ray got to her house he snuck up to a side window and peaked in. I couldn't see what he was looking at so I moved in a little closer. When I looked into the window I could see Sara standing next to a mirror butt naked. I was so embarrassed and ashamed I turned away and ran into the woods as fast as I could and Billy Ray was right behind me laughing his head off.

"What's da matter Jeremiah, ain't choo ever seen a naked gal befoe?"

"Naw Billy Ray, I ain't, what about choo?"

"I see em all da time Jeremiah, sometimes I go down to da river and I see white girls swimmin in dey under pants."

"You mean you be lookin at em, Billy Ray?"

"I sho do, and dey know's I be lookin. I think dey like's it."

"Why you do dat Billy Ray?"

"Cause it feels good, now come on lets go back down there."

"I ain't going nowhere, dats not right Billy Ray, peakin in gal's windows and watchin em swim in dey under pants and such."

"I see you still a scary cat, Jeremiah."

"I ain't no scary cat Billy Ray, dat's jest not right."

"She don't care, dat girl been walkin round at night naked as a jay bird fo years, she knows I be lookin."

"How da you know she don't care Billy Ray?"

"Cause I been comin down here since last summer and one time she caught me lookin and she didn't tell her momma or da sheriff."

"Dat don't mean she know you still keep comin Billy Ray."

"Yes she do, cause after dat time she caught me, I came back and she was doin da same thang. Now dat don't seem like a gal dat don't want to be watched. Dis time when I finish lookin at her, I'm gonna climb into her room and I bet choo she let me have my way wit her," he said with a strange smile.

"You a lie Billy Ray, dat gal to high and mighty actin, she ain't gonna let choo have yo way wit her!"

"Dey always do Jeremiah, don't be so ignorant."

"You mean you do dis all da time, Billy Ray?"

"Yep, and if you don't believe me come on back down there and I'll let choo watch. Dey always let me have my way wit em!"

Billy Ray led the way and I followed. When we got back to Sara's window she was still walking around her room butt naked. Billy Ray watched for a while but I was to ashamed, even though a part of me really did want to look. Sara put on her night gown, turned out the light and went to bed. Billy Ray quickly climbed through her window and jumped on top of her. He whispered something in her ear and she didn't scream or make a sound she just laid there as Billy Ray Horton had his way with her. Maybe it was consensual between the two of them and maybe it wasn't. I didn't know what to do, but I felt I had to do something so when Billy Ray came back out the window, I dragged him into the woods and beat the mess out of him. I stomped and kicked him until I was to tired to keep on. After I finished whuppin his butt, I said to him, "You must be crazy Billy Ray, you ain't got no right comin to New Bethlehem and do dis to a colored gal. You know you wouldn't get away wit doing dis to a white gal."

"It ain't what choo thank Jeremiah," he pleaded. "It ain't what choo thank!"

"If I ever catch you doin somethin like this again I'll finish what I started."

I left Billy Ray laying in the woods and we didn't speak for along time after that. About eight or nine months later Sara had a baby and that baby was as white as snow with hazel eyes to match. Some folk say that the baby looked white because Sara's granddaddy was white but I thought I knew the truth. Over the next few years several young colored girls were attacked and raped in their own rooms, and some eventually had babies. All those babies looked white but nobody made much fuss, I suppose everyone suspected the daddy of all those children was white, but they were all to afraid to talk about it let alone come forward. For years colored folk kept their doors locked and closed the shutters on their daughters windows at night but some unknown man continued attacking and raping colored girls in New Bethlehem.

Nobody was ever caught but I suppose it didn't really matter because it was just colored girls getting attacked, at least that's how the sheriff saw it. I know one thing for sure, if it had been white girls getting attacked and raped everybody and their momma would have been screaming bloody murder. I don't know for sure, but I don't think what Billy Ray did to Sara James was friendly relations.

Chapter 7

Vanished

One Sunday morning Reverend Hightower made an announcement. He told the congregation that sixteen year old Mary Houston had been missing for three days. He said she was last seen walking down Old Miller road wearing a pretty pink dress with patent leather shoes and white stocking. She was on her way to her grandmother's house for a visit but she never showed up. He also told us that he planned to go to Burdonville later that day and tell the sheriff what's been going on in New Bethlehem. My brother's and I went with my daddy, the Reverend and the other men to town that day. When we arrived in Burdonville I was shocked when I saw Billy Ray wearing a sheriff's badge and uniform. Billy Ray was the sheriff's new deputy and he was as smug and arrogant as ever. He had suspicious looking scratches all over his neck and arms and when we approached the jail he nervously stepped forward and asked us what we wanted.

"What can I do for ya'll?" he asked nervously.

"We come to see the sheriff Billy Ray," said Reverend Hightower.

"It's deputy Horton, preacher," said Billy Ray.

Reverend Hightower paused for a moment then looked Billy Ray right in the eyes as he walked right up to him. Billy Ray was very nervous and he started stuttering.

"Where did you get those scratches deputy Horton?" asked the Reverend.

"Ahhh,,,,ahhh,,,a wild cat. The sheriff's out back sleep, what can I do for ya?"

"We would appreciate it very much if you would go out back and wake him up."

"Jest tell me what da problem is, I'll see if I can help."

"I think you should tend to those scratches, then go get the sheriff, deputy."

The whole town must have gathered around that old jail by that time, women and children included. I suppose those white folk ain't never seen so many colored men gathered together walking down the main street like that before, it sure was a sight. Billy Ray nervously went out back to get the sheriff. When the sheriff came to the front of the jail he looked as nervous as Billy Ray. A white man standing across the street yelled out,

"Is everythang alright sheriff?"

"Everythang's jest fine Homer," he said. "Now what can I do for ya'll?"

"Sheriff, young Mary Houston has been missing for three days."

"Is dat right?" he said.

"Yes sa, and we want you to do something about it."

"Well, I don't know what I can do bout it, she probably done run off wit some young colored buck, and dey out havin a good time."

"No sa, that ain't the case sheriff," said Reverend Hightower. "Mary wouldn't run off and leave her momma, sheriff."

"Now what makes you so sure Reverend?"

"Cause she didn't take none of her belongings."

"Now dat don't mean nothin, maybe she was in to big a hurry to pack."

"That ain't all we come to talk to you about sheriff."

"What else is it Reverend?" he said. "I'm a busy man."

"Well sa, somebody been coming down to New Bethlehem after dark, and attacking colored gals."

"Is dat all Reverend, now you know as well as I do, that dem young bucks down in New Bethlehem can't control dey urges and such."

"Well this ain't the case sheriff, cause some of them gals came up pregnant."

"Well last I checked, that is what happens when a boy and a gal gets together."

Suddenly Billy Ray and the whole town started laughing out loud. I couldn't bring myself to say I thought it was Billy Ray attacking all them colored girls even though the sheriff was trying to make a fool out of Reverend Hightower, and for a moment it was working until Mr. Washington yelled out,

"Yea, but dem babies look white!"

Suddenly you could hear a pen drop it was so quiet. White folks slowly started mumbling all around us.

"What choo say boy?"

"I ain't no boy sheriff, and I said, dem babies all came out lookin white."

"So ya'll saying a white man coming down yonda and rapin dem colored gals?"

"No sa, we ain't saying no such thang," said Reverend Hightower. "We just want you to find the man that's responsible for hurting our women folk, that's all sheriff, we don't want no trouble."

"Looks like ya'll want some trouble to me," said the sheriff. "Ya'll come to town like a pack of wolves and actin like ya'll was gonna do somethin."

"No sa, we don't want no trouble, we just want some help."

"Well, I'll tell you how I'm gonna help ya," he said. "I'm gonna give you the best advice I can. Ya'll turn right around and carry yo colored butts right back out of town and go home befoe I throw all ya'll into jail for makin false accusations on a white man."

"Sheriff, we ain't never said it was no white man, we jest said da babies looked white, dat's all," said Mr. Brown.

"Now ya'll got about five minutes to get out of town, or go to jail."

With all the white folks in town watching we turned around and left. We were humiliated and embarrassed but not discouraged. When we got out of town we gathered at the sight of the old church that had burned down several years before. Reverend Hightower told all the men that the only way we were going to find Mary Houston was to search ourselves. We spread out all over New Bethlehem and searched the fields and the woods. We must have searched all night but we didn't find her anywhere.

Right before dusk the next day Reverend Hightower sent word for all the men to gather at the sight of the old church again. He told us that while we were out searching for Mary another colored girl had been raped. He told us he had a plan to catch the rapist. He told us to split up into small groups and hide quietly in the woods near every colored girls house in New Bethlehem. The plan was to try and catch him in the act. We took turns hiding in the woods for months, but we never did catch him. It was as though who ever he was he knew every move we were gonna make before we made it.

Chapter 8

The Surprise

Several years have passed and it was now 1933 and I was no longer a boy, I was an eighteen year old man. The town was already divided by race and class and it seemed normal for white folks to blame colored folk for all their problems and for colored folk to blame white folks for all their problems. If a cow wondered off some white folks farm it was assumed that a colored man must have stolen it or if some chickens or hogs went missing the first place white folks would look would be the nearest colored farm. I suppose colored folk did the same thing the only difference was the fact that if a white farmer did steal something from a colored farmer there wasn't nothing the colored farmer could do about it. Billy Ray Horton had been involved in all kinds of mischief and trouble over the past ten years and as far as white folks were concerned it was mostly harmless, good old fashioned fun.

Colored folk used to tell me to stay away from Billy Ray, and Billy Ray once told me that white folks told him to stay away from me. I don't know if that was true but even white folks had to know that Billy Ray was bad news even if he was the sheriff's deputy. One afternoon my daddy sent me to town for some flower, sugar and salt. As I walked through town I could feel the stares and hostility from the white folks. They were looking at me as if I had committed a crime or something. I went straight to the country store and waited my turn for Mr. Timble to wait on me. As usual he took his time and made me wait at least an hour before he asked me what I wanted.

"What choo want boy," he said with a deep southern drawl.

"I need some sugar, salt and flower, sa," I said.

He stared at me with so much contempt and hate in his eyes I almost decided to walk out but I knew I didn't do anything wrong so I just stood my ground and patiently waited.

"How much choo want, boy?"

"I need two pounds of sugar, two pounds of flower and two pounds of salt."

"You got enough money fo all dis, boy?"

"Yes sa, my daddy gave me one dollar," I said confidently.

"Where yo daddy get dat kinda money boy?" he said. "He steal it?" he asked.

"No sa, my daddy ain't no thief, he sharecrops on Mr. Horton's land."

"Oh yea, now I know who you is, you Matthew Liggon's boy," he said.

"Yes sa, I'm Jeremiah Liggons."

"Yea,,,,you da one dat Billy Ray say been peekin in all dem colored gals bedrooms when dey ain't got no clothes on. What dem gals look like naked boy?" he said.

"I ain't never seen em naked sa, I ain't never peeked in no window neither."

"Sho you did boy. I bet choo like sneakin round in dem woods, waitin fo it to get dark, so you can climb in dey windows and have yo way wit em. Dem colored gals probably like yo black, greasy butt, don't dey?"

"No sa, dat ain't true, I ain't never did no such thang," I said. At that point Mr. Timble got very angry and started yelling at me.

"What choo say boy, you callin deputy Horton a liar?"

"No sa, I ain't callin nobody no liar sa, I jest thank he must be mistaken."

"You betta not be callin deputy Horton a liar boy, cause if you is, you be in big trouble, you hear me boy?"

"Yes sa, I wouldn't dare call Billy Ray, I mean deputy Horton a liar, no sa."

"You betta not and you best keep to peeking in dem colored gals rooms cause if you try peeking in a white gals room you gonna get hung. You hear me boy?"

"Yes sa!"

Mr. Timble finished putting my salt, sugar and flour in small bags all the while giving me dirty looks. I couldn't help but think that after all I'd been through with Billy Ray that he had the nerve to go around town telling white folks that I was the one peeking into colored girls rooms. When I left Mr. Timble's country store I went straight to the jail to confront Billy Ray but on the way to the jail I started thinking about the fact that me and Billy Ray weren't children anymore.

We were both eighteen years old and I could get thrown into jail or worse if I showed any amount of disrespect even to Billy Ray. When I started to leave town I saw Billy Ray coming out of the town bar. He stopped and stared at me for a moment as I walked by but he didn't say a word. When I got to the edge of town I turned around and looked back toward the bar and he was still standing there staring at me. Suddenly, for the first time in years, back to the time I saw Billy Ray killing small animals, I felt a strange fear. I felt like I was being watched by evil itself. When I got home my whole family had gathered around the kitchen table to surprise me.

"Sit down Jeremiah, I got somethin I want to tell you," said daddy.

"What's wrong daddy?"

"Nothin son, yo momma and I decided it was time dat choo went away."

"Ya'll sendin me away, but I didn't do nothin daddy, I promise I'll work harder," I pleaded.

"Jeremiah, listen son, we sendin you to college."

"College?" I said.

"Yes, college. Reverend Hightower wrote a letter to a colored college in Atlanta on yo behalf. Dat college is fo colored boys and dey say you welcome. You always did get good marks in school, and you da smartest colored boy in town."

"But daddy, it cost to much."

"Don't choo worry bout dat, you jest pack yo belongins and get ready to go."

"You mean I got's to leave now?"

"First thang in da mornin, school be startin in two days."

All my brothers and sisters congratulated me. They hugged and kissed me till I couldn't take it no more. Later that night I went out to the porch where my daddy was sitting in his rocking chair, smoking his wooden pipe and momma was reading her bible under the moon light. I remember the fire flies buzzing around like embers from a fire and I could hear the crickets and owls singing in the night. That night it seemed like every star in the universe was as bright as the sun and the moon looked like I could just reach out and touch it. I don't know how my daddy and momma was able to save up enough money to send me to college, especially because there was nine of us youngins but they did. I was determined to make them all proud no matter what.

I always dreamed of going to college but I never thought I'd get the opportunity and now my dreams were about to come true. I sat with momma and daddy out on the porch for hours, nobody said a word, it was as though we could read each others minds. The next morning I was all packed and ready to take the long walk to the train station when my daddy pulled up in front of the house with that old mule and wagon. He was wearing his only suit and he had a big smile on his face.

"Well, what choo waitin on? Hop on, dat train ain't gonna wait for no man."

"I can walk daddy, you've done enough fo me already, it's time I took responsibility fo myself."

"Well, well, well, you ain't even got to college yet, and you already growin up."

"Daddy, all I ever wanted to do was make you and momma proud of me."

"I know dat son, we already proud of you. You know you da first one in dis family to finish grade school, now you gonna be da first one to go to college. Why do you think I never made you work in dem fields wit the rest of us son."

"Cause I was to scrawny and weak?"

"Naw, dat ain't it son. From da time you could crawl you was turning dem pages of yo momma's bible like you was readin. Me and yo momma knew we had somethin special right then and there. We decided to give you different kinds of chores to keep you busy cause we knew your head was gonna always be in dem books. You got a gift son, a gift from da good Lord and it's time you found out what dat gift is. Me and yo momma done taught you all we know, we can't teach choo nuttin else. You have to go the rest of da way by yourself."

"Ya'll gonna leave me alone daddy?"

"Naw son, we ain't never gonna leave you, we always gonna be wit choo in spirit. Now get on dis wagon fo you miss da train."

Just then my momma came out of the house in her pretty yellow dress. She looked as beautiful as a Sunday morning.

"Now I know ya'll wasn't fixin to leave without me," she said. "My baby goin off to college on da train, and I means to see he makes it safely."

"Well climb on board Mrs. Liggons," my daddy said with a big smile.

"Let me help you up momma," I said.

"Well thank you kindly, Jeremiah," she said.

I climbed into the back of the wagon and took a long hard look at that little house because I knew wasn't going to see it again for a long time. As we started to leave I felt tears roll down the side of my face. As we rode down by the fields where my brothers and sisters were working they all dropped their cotton sacks and came running toward the dirt road. Daddy stopped for a moment so they could all say good bye.

"Take care of yourself Jeremiah," said my oldest sister Kathyren.

"Remember who you is Jeremiah," said my brother Mark.

"Don't take no stuff from dem uppity colored folk up at dat college," said my brother John.

"We loves you Jeremiah, and we sho nuff proud a you," said my sister Mary.

"Don't choo stay out at night, member you sposed to be learnin," said my brother James."

"I suppose we ain't gonna have no catfish fo a long time," said my brother Abraham. "I done ate so much catfish I do believe I'm starting to look like one."

"You got some clean draws Jeremiah," asked my sister Cleo.

"You betta not come back here wit no wife and babies Jeremiah, you hear me?" said my sister Lula.

We all laughed and hugged each other. I knew I was gonna miss my family more than words could say, so I just smiled. We continued down Old Miller road headed for town and I stared at my brothers and sisters until they were to small to see in the distance. As we traveled down that road I started thinking back to the time that Billy Ray stole those apples from Mr. Johnson and how I was the one that got in trouble for it. I laughed for a while, then I remembered how scared I was, then I felt like crying but I didn't.

When we arrived in town that morning we went straight to the train station. As we traveled through town all the White folks seemed to stop and stare at us. I remember thinking that everything seemed to be moving in slow motion and as usual I could feel their contempt and hatred deep down inside. It was as if their eyes pierced my body like bullets. When we arrived at the train station my daddy stopped the wagon and came around to the side and helped my momma down.

My momma moved very graciously, like a woman with culture and class. She held her head high as she stepped down from that old wagon still holding my daddy's hand. When she stepped down from that wagon she put her hand in daddy's arm and they casually, yet with purpose, walked into the colored entrance of the train station to buy my ticket. I quickly jumped out of that wagon and grabbed my belongings. I paused for a moment and stared back at those White folks who were staring at me. After standing there on the steps of the train station for a while I turned around and went inside but before I made it all the way in I suddenly realized I entered the white's Only entrance.

"What choo thank you doin boy?" yelled the station attendant. "Can't choo read, dat sign say white entrance!"

"I'm sorry sa," I stuttered. "I wasn't paying attention."

"Well you betta start payin attention boy, fo you find yoself in a world a hurt."

"Yes sa!" I said.

My daddy turned around and stared at that attendant so hard I thought he was going to say something, but I could see my momma holding his arm as tight as she could to hold him back. My daddy was grinding his teethe and breathing heavy through his nose. I don't ever recall my daddy being so angry not even the time me and Billy Ray Horton burned down the church, but he didn't say a word to the station attendant, he just told me to come and stand next to him and momma.

"Come stand over here son."

"Yes sa," I said.

"You know betta den to come through dat door, what was you thinkin?" he whispered.

"I don't know daddy."

"Jeremiah, you on yo way to college and you can't afford to make no mistakes."

"I know daddy, I'm sorry."

"You don't have to be sorry son, jest be careful," he said.

"Yes sa."

Daddy turned around to the counter to pay for my ticket and started talking to the colored station attendant.

"How you doin Matthew?"

"I'm jest fine Harold, I needs one ticket to Atlanta."

"Why you goin to Atlanta Matthew, somebody pass away up yonda?"

"Naw Harold, my youngest boy Jeremiah goin off to college," he said with pride.

"College?" he said. "Well don't dat beat all."

Just then, in the middle of their conversation, the white station attendant came over to my daddy and said,

"Is you gonna buy a ticket or not, boy?"

"Boy?" my daddy asked.

"You heard me. I know who you is Matthew Liggons, you dat uppity nigga dat sharecrops on Horton's farm," he said. "You thank you betta than da rest of dem niggas but let me tell you somethin, you ain't. You ain't nothin but a low down dirty nigga and dats all any of ya'll ever gonna be," he said with anger. My daddy very calmly, under complete control, and with a big smile on his face turned to him and said, "Yes sa, I suppose your right."

I was shocked and amazed. I was expecting my daddy to punch that old white man right in the nose but he didn't. That old white man just stood there with a blank look on his face, I suppose he was expecting my daddy to punch him too. He stood there for a moment then went back to the white's only counter. It took several years before I understood that my daddy out smarted that old white man by using reverse psychology. My daddy made a fool out of him without getting himself hung. I reckon if that white man knew what my daddy was doing he would have had him strung up to the nearest tree without thinking a second thought about it. During this whole ordeal my momma was very calm and prayerful. She just stood there and smiled at me. Her eyes were filled with pride and love.

"Jeremiah, when you get to school, I wants you to write and tell us how you doin, you hear?" said momma.

"Yes ma'am."

"And don't forget to say your prayers at night and in da mornin, you hear?"

"Yes ma'am."

"And don't get mixed up wit dem fast gals from da city, you hear?"

"Yes ma'am."

"And keep yo clothes clean, and take a bath everyday," she said. "And don't forget to write a letter to Reverend Hightower and thank him fo what he did."

"Yes ma'am, I will momma."

After my daddy got my ticket we all went out to wait on the train. As we sat and talked about college and such, I caught a glimpse of Billy Ray watching us from his police car down the main street. When he saw me looking at him he slowly put his hand out the window and waved good bye.

I reluctantly waved back, after which, he slowly drove away. I often wondered how Billy Ray knew I was going off to college, after all, I only found out the night before. I reckon it was like everything else that goes on in a small town, everybody knows your business before you do.

"ALL ABOARD!" the conductor yelled.

"Bye momma, I love you."

"Bye Jeremiah, I love you too son. Don't forget to call on da Lord if'n you get into trouble son. Take care of yourself, and remember what I said, you hear!"

"I will momma. Bye daddy, thanks for everythin."

"Take good care of yourself son, and remember who you is."

"I will daddy, I won't ever forget. I love you daddy."

"I loves you too son."

"ALL ABOARD," the conductor yelled.

"I'll make you proud, I promise," I yelled.

"We're already proud son. We're already proud," said my daddy.

"Dear Lord in heaven, thank you fo the heavenly Angel you sent forth to watch over our family, and I pray in the name of Jesus that you send an Angel right along with our son Jeremiah to watch over him all the days of his life. Protect him dear Lord from all hurt or harm and help him to make the right decisions and to always do the right thing, in Jesus name I pray, Amen," prayed momma.

As the train started to pull away I stood on the steps of the colored only car and waved to my momma and daddy until I couldn't see them anymore. I thought about momma's prayer and how powerful it was the first time I heard it back when I was a youngin. I never told my momma that I had already seen and heard an Angel, but like everything else that happened in New Bethlehem, I'm sure momma already knew.

Chapter 9

College

Riding on that train to Atlanta I saw mansions, farms, rivers and fancy cars all along the way. I felt like I was leaving one world and entering another and in many ways, I was. I saw colored folk with their Sunday go to meeting clothes on and it wasn't even Sunday, this was the best surprise I ever had. I saw fancy new cars all over the place, and the colored women were wearing big fancy hats and holding those little umbrella's like the ones I'd seen at the Horton's party several years before. It was at that moment that I knew my life would never again be the same. The colored folk in Atlanta looked as prosperous as white folk. I couldn't believe my eyes but I had to. There they were big as life and dressed so fine. There were colored folk running business's, going to work in office buildings as tall as the sky. And there wasn't a dirt road to be found and not a cotton field in sight. This was truly a new world that I was entering and though I was a little apprehensive I welcomed the opportunity with the utmost optimism.

    I arrived at Scripture College in Atlanta about 3:00 that Saturday afternoon and I never felt so lost in all my life. I walked around campus for a while looking for the deans office but I couldn't find it. I didn't want to ask anyone for help because I didn't want to look like a country bumpkin. I suppose all it took was one look at me and any idiot could tell I was fresh off the farm. I was carrying one tote bag with one pair of socks, some drawers, one under shirt, some long johns and a wash rag.

I was wearing my brother Abraham's pants that were to big, my brother James's shirt that was to big and my brother Mark's black leather shoes that were way to big. The only thing I was wearing that fit properly was a pair of white cotton socks that belonged to my sister Kathyren. Looking back in retrospect, I must have looked like a clown from the circus but to tell you the truth I didn't care, I was just happy to be there. As I continued searching for the deans office a tall slender well dressed colored man walked up to me and looked me over like I was a prize hog or something. He walked around me checking out my clothes and shaking his head.

"What's your major country boy?" he asked.

"My what?" I asked.

"Your major," you know, what are you going to study?"

"Oh,,,I want to be a school teacher," I said.

"A teacher, where are you going to teach, country boy?" he asked.

"My name is not country boy, it's Jeremiah, Jeremiah Liggons, and I plan on teaching back home in New Bethlehem," I said with pride.

"Excuse me, country boy, I mean Jeremiah Liggons, I didn't mean to offend you," he said. "My name is Martin Norwood. I'm going to be an engineer."

"Please to meet choo Martin Norwood."

"What do you got in that tote bag, Jeremiah?" he asked.

"Jest my personal affects," I said.

"Well, I hope you have some clothes that fit better than what you have on."

"As a matter of fact, these is da only clothes I got. My brothers and sisters gave em to me," I said with pride.

"Well, I didn't mean to offend you Jeremiah, but you can't expect to meet any girls with those big old clothes on," he said.

"Well, fo yo information, I didn't come all dis way to meet no gals, we got gals back home in New Bethlehem," I said. "I comes to get an education."

"Ain't nothing wrong with getting an education, that's what we're all here for. But there show is some fine looking gals around here," he said with a smile.

"My daddy said dis was a college fo colored boys, ain't no gals sposed to be here."

"You sho are country ain't choo. The gals ain't on this campus, they're at Virtue College across the street. Come on Jeremiah I can see now I got to show you the ropes," he said.

What a strange way to introduce yourself to someone I thought. But I suppose it must have been the custom in college. Where I come from people just walk up to you and say "hey, my name is so and so, what's yours?" During my first year of college it seemed as though I was always getting lost, but low and behold, Martin was always there to help me out. Everyone was friendly and helpful, especially the professors. I was very impressed with the professors and the way they spoke. Their English was what I considered to be very proper. I worked hard to lose my country drawl, or accent if you will, but it wasn't easy. My first courses were math, English, science, history, literature and geography.

It was tough in the beginning, but I ultimately received good marks in all my class's. I knew how difficult it was going to be for momma and daddy to send me money every month for tuition and living expenses, so I got a part time job down at the local market bagging groceries, stocking shelves, and running errands. That little job didn't pay very much, but it was a real big help to momma and daddy. During the summer months when school was out, the dean allowed me to stay on campus in the dormitory free of charge, just so I could keep working. It was a lonely existence during the summer.

Everyone was gone and every once in a while I thought I heard someone walking the halls at night. Every little noise was elevated because of the silence and I often imagined hearing laughter down the dark, empty corridors. So, to make up for my loneliness, I worked a second job loading trucks at night. By the time I got back to the dormitory I was to sleepy to hear any strange noises. Eventually I saved up enough money to send a little home as well as keep some for new books, food, and clothes. Martin and I became good friends and I learned a great deal about life from him.

Several years have passed since I first went to college, and at the age of twenty two, I was in my last semester of my senior year. I was still working at the little market which had grown to be a large grocery store, when one day while reading the local colored paper, I read an article about colored girls getting raped in the middle of the night back in New Bethlehem. I couldn't believe it was still going on. And to make matters worse, I was stunned when I read that the new sheriff in town was Billy Ray Horton. Billy Ray had worked his way up to sheriff from deputy in three years, partly because sheriff Banks drank too much corn liquor and one day just dropped dead.

I started thinking back to when Billy Ray and I were children and the pact we made with each other to always protect each other and keep each other's secrets as long as we lived. But now we were no longer children, and the bible says in 1 Corinthians 13:11,"*When I was a child, I spoke as a child, I understood as a child, I thought as a child; but when I became a man, I put away childish things.*" With that in mind I knew I would ultimately have to confront my past and Billy Ray Horton. As my senior year wound down I looked forward to my graduation ceremony even though my family couldn't afford to come. After the ceremony Martin and I were talking about his plans to build bridges, buildings and colored towns all over the country. After we received our degree's from the dean, Martin came running up to me like a child in a candy store and as I remember he was so excited and filled with hope for the future.

"Hey Jeremiah, what's the good word?" he said with a smile.

"I was just thinking Martin."

"Thinking?" he said. "Man, that's all we have been doing for the past four years is thinking."

"Yea I know, but I was thinking about New Bethlehem and all the colored children back home," I said. "I just wish my momma and daddy could have been here to see me walk across that stage and get my degree."

"I know how you feel, my family couldn't afford to come here from Alabama to see me graduate either. Well, at least they'll see your degree when you get home, because the main thing is you got it!"

"That's true," I said. "Hey Martin, what are you going to do now that you have your degree in engineering and architecture?"

"I'm going to design and build bridges and buildings all over the world."

"That sounds great Martin, where are you going to start?" I asked.

"Well, I hadn't worked that part out yet. I was thinking about California."

"California sounds good Martin, but tell me something. Shouldn't you start right here in Georgia, you know, get some experience?" I asked.

"Hmm,,,,,,,,,,,I suppose your right," he said.

"Good, I got just the place for you to get all the experience you need," I said.

"What are you talking about Jeremiah?"

"I'm talking about New Bethlehem."

"New Bethlehem?" he said. "What kind of experience can I get in New Bethlehem?"

"I'm glad you asked that Martin," I said with a smile. "The colored folk in New Bethlehem don't have a church to go to since the old burned down along time ago and the children don't have a school.

"Jeremiah, that sort of thing cost a whole lot of money, the kind of money we don't have," he said.

"That may be true, but we got faith. My momma always said, if you have faith it can move mountains."

"But where are we gonna get the supplies such as lumber, nails, saws, hammers and paint?" asked Martin.

"Oh ye of little faith," I said with a smile. "New Bethlehem has more abandoned farm house's and barns than I can shake a stick at. All that lumber ain't doing nothing but rotten in the sun."

"I don't know Jeremiah, seems like a lot of hard work to me."

"Now I know Martin Norwood ain't afraid of a little hard work!" I said sarcastically.

"Who me, hard work is my middle name, as a matter of fact my full name is Martin 'Hard Work' Norwood. "

"Is that right?" I said.

"That's right!"

"So will you do it?" I asked.

"Well, I suppose California can wait a few months," he said with a big smile.

We laughed for a while then walked around congratulating our class mates. Later that afternoon we went to the dormitory to pack. I couldn't wait to see my family back home and I knew they were really going to be surprised when they found out we were going to build a new school and a church for the colored folk in New Bethlehem. As I prepared to leave college and go home my head was full of hopes, dreams, and ideas, and I carried in my hand a brand new college degree.

Chapter 10

Welcome Home

While riding the train back home I felt as though I was in some type of time machine going back into time. I had lived and worked in Atlanta for over three years and I suppose in many ways I had become a part of the city. The big city with it's bright lights, excitement, cars and trains that were moving all hours of the day and night had become normal to me. In stark contrast, New Bethlehem was slow, quiet and laid back. My friend Martin came home with me to build a new church and school in New Bethlehem but to this day I don't think he knew what he was getting into. When we arrived in Burdonville it was immediately apparent that nothing had changed with the exception of paved roads in town. It was as if I never left and in some ways it appears as though time simply stood still. We got off the train and started walking down the main street toward New Bethlehem.

"This don't look like the New Bethlehem you described to me Jeremiah," said Martin. "I don't see nothing but white folk, where's all those beautiful young colored gals you been telling me about?"

"This ain't New Bethlehem, this here is Burdonville." I said. "New Bethlehem is down that road."

As we walked through town white folks stopped what they were doing and stared at us, but we knew better than to say anything or even look back at them so we just kept walking. No sooner than we left town we found ourselves walking on dirt roads. I wasn't quite sure but I thought I caught a glimpse of Billy Ray watching us leave town. Maybe it was my imagination or just instinct, I don't no for sure but the last time I saw Billy Ray a strange kind of evil seemed to have a hold of him. We walked for about thirty minutes down Old Miller road before we got to the place where the old church once stood. The ashes and burnt cinder blocks were still there, a kind of eerie reminder of my past. We stopped at the edge of the church grounds for a moment and I told Martin about what had happened there so long ago.

"Looks like the klan been up to no good around here Jeremiah," he said. "You didn't tell me ya'll had problems with the klan."

"No Martin, this wasn't done by the klan," I said.

"What are you talking about, this was a church wasn't it?" he said. "I can see the grave yard right over there."

"Yea this was a church, but the klan didn't burn it down, we did."

"What did you say Jeremiah, we did, who was we?"

"It's a long story Martin."

"Well you got me all the way down here from Atlanta to build a church, don't you think you better tell me who, we is?" he asked.

"It was a accident. Me and Billy Ray tried smoking cigarettes one summer, and we wound up coughing and choking, so needless to say we threw the lit cigarettes on the ground near the church and walked away. A little while later the church was on fire. It was an accident," I said. "Do you believe in Angels Martin?"

"What?"

"Do you believe in Angels?"

",,I suppose so,,,yea,,the good book says there are such things as Angels, why?"

",,I was just wondering that's all."

We stood there for a while looking at what was left of the old church before we headed home. Along the way we ran into my brothers and sisters coming in from the fields.

"Is dat choo Jeremiah?" asked my sister Kathyren.

"Jeremiah?" asked my brother Mark.

"Yes em, it's me, I'm home," I said.

At that moment they all gathered around me and started hugging and kissing me. We laughed and hugged for what seemed like hours. At that moment I realized they missed me as much as I missed them. In the middle of all the hugs and kiss's I almost forgot to introduce them to Martin.

"This here is my good friend Martin."

They all stopped hugging me and slowly started gathering around Martin. He looked as though he had seen a ghost as they slowly closed in around him.

"So this is Martin. You da one dat talked about my baby brothers clothes when he first got to dat college?" Abraham said sarcastically.

"I,,,I,,,I didn't mean no harm,,, I was just having a little fun with Jeremiah," he said nervously.

"We don't take kindly to uppity colored folk talkin down to our kin folk," Abraham said in deep voice.

"Yeap, we show don't take kindly to no uppity colored folk talkin down to our kin folk," said my brother John.

"Do you know what we done to da last uppity colored man dat tried dat?" asked my sister Mary. "We grabbed em round da neck,,,,,,,,,,and started huggin and kissin em."

Then suddenly everyone started laughing and hugging him. Martin was very nervous and he looked as though he was about to take off running. They got a real big laugh out of that and so did Martin after he saw they were only having fun with him.

"Hey Martin, nice to meet choo, I'm Lula, Jeremiah's older sister.

"Yea, nice to meet choo there Martin, I'm Mark, Jeremiah's older brother.

"What's wrong wit choo boy, you look like you done went and messed in yo pants,"Abraham said laughingly. "I'm Abraham, Jeremiah's oldest brother.

"Hey Martin, I'm Kathyren, Jeremiah's oldest sister."

"I'm Cleo, me and Jeremiah are da youngest," she said with a smile.

"And I'm Mary, I'm Jeremiah's older sister also."

"How you doin Martin, I'm James, Jeremiah's older brother."

After everyone introduced themselves to Martin we started walking home. Martin and Cleo kept smiling at each other as we walked, and it became obvious that they were attracked to each other.

"Where's daddy?" I asked.

"He up to da house, he been feelin poorly lately," said Abraham.

"But he sho gonna feel good when he see you Jeremiah," said Kathyren.

When we got near the edge of the farm I could smell my momma's fried chicken, corn bread, collard greens, black eyed peas, and sweet potato pie. I knew I was home. Momma used to cook like that all the time and for some folks that was a special Sunday meal but around my house momma cooked like that everyday. Daddy was sitting out on the porch rocking in his chair and smoking his wooden pipe when we got to the house. Everybody stopped out in the yard and I slowly approached alone. When daddy saw that it was me he stopped rocking and slowly stood up.

He walked to the edge of the porch holding on to the post. He didn't move as quickly as he used to and for the first time in my life my daddy looked old. He had rivers of wrinkles on his face that looked like dark canyons and his hair was gray like day old coals from a fire. He reached out to me and I could see the years of hard labor all over his massive hands. I looked into his eyes and I saw a life time of pain, suffering and pride, all rolled up into one, as tears flowed down his face.

"Hey daddy," I said.

"Welcome home son," he said. "Come on up here and let me take a look at choo."

I walked up to the porch and embraced my daddy for the first time in almost four years. When I left this place I called home I was a scrawny, nappy haired boy filled with dreams and when I returned I was a man with a vision.

"Thank you daddy, it feels good to be home."

As I stood there hugging my daddy, my momma came out on the porch. She was already crying tears of joy when she saw me.

I couldn't believe my eyes, momma looked as though she hadn't aged one day. Her hair was like brown gold, rich, shiny and full of life. Her beautiful cream colored skin seemed to glow in the late evening sun and her tears sparkled like a river of diamonds. She moved with the grace of royalty as she embraced me and daddy at the same time.

"My baby is home," she said with pride.

"Hey momma," I said.

"Thank you Jesus,,,,thank you Jesus,,, my baby is home," she cried.

Chapter 11

Mary Houston

On the night I returned home from college, my whole family sat out on the porch with me after supper. We talked and laughed for hours. It was as though I never left. Every once in a while there would be complete silence, with the exception of a barn owl singing at the moon, and the crickets playing back up. For a time the peace and quiet was as welcome as life it self, and for a minute, I even missed the city, for a minute. While we were sitting there talking about old times, we could see the head lights of a car coming down Old Miller road. Word had spread that I was home and Reverend Hightower wanted to come over and congratulate me on graduating from college and see how I was doing. As he got out of the car he walked with a slight limp, and as usual he had his old worn out bible with him.

"Good evening Reverend," said my daddy.

"Good evening everybody," he said as he slowly walked up to the porch.

"Good evening Reverend," said my momma.

"Well, well, well,,,,the blessed son has returned," said the Reverend. "Stand up Jeremiah and let me take a look at you."

"How are you doing Reverend?" I asked. "Momma tells me you have taken ill."

"I'm just fine Jeremiah, just fine," he said.

"Don't he sound different Reverend?" said Abraham. "He sounds like white folks don't he?"

"I reckon he does at that."

"He talks like a educated man," John said with a smile.

"Sit down Reverend, take some weight off dem feet," said daddy. "James, get up and give da Reverend a chair.

"Thank you James, thank you," said the Reverend. "Jeremiah, did you learn anything up at Scripture College?" asked the Reverend.

"Yes sir, I learned a great deal," I said with pride.

"What are you going to do with all that learning Jeremiah?" he asked.

"I plan on teaching Reverend."

"A school teacher?"

"Yes sir, right here in New Bethlehem."

"Well praise the Lord," he said. "The children around here need a good teacher."

"Well I don't know if I'll be as good as you were Reverend."

"Oh, thank you Jeremiah, but you'll be a whole lot better than I ever was. You know, I never made it past the six grade," he said. "I taught myself after that. You are going to be the first real teacher any of these children around here have ever seen."

"I just want to do a good job Reverend."

"I'm sure you will Jeremiah, I'm sure you will."

"Excuse me for my manners Reverend, I almost forgot. I want you to meet my good friend Martin Norwood. Martin is going to help me build a school and a church."

Before I could utter another word everyone on the porch started talking all at once. They couldn't believe what they heard.

"What did you say Jeremiah," asked daddy.

"Martin is going to help me build a school and a church."

"Dat's what I thought choo said," said daddy. "Do you have any idea how much somethin like dat cost?"

"A school, where you gonna get da money to build a school Jeremiah?" asked momma.

"Well, me and Martin have it all worked out," I said.

"Is that what choo learned up to dat college Jeremiah?" asked daddy. "Is dat what dey teaches up there, foolishness?"

"No sir, it ain't foolishness daddy. It can be done and it won't cost a penny," I said.

"Boy you must be crazy, where da money gonna come from?" asked James.

"Well, the way I figured it, you know all those abandoned farms and barns down Old Miller road, and up around Pickens road?" I asked. "Those places are just sitting and rotten in the sun right. Don't nobody want them old places, but I reckon the wood and nails can be put to some good use."

"That's a wonderful idea Jeremiah," said the Reverend. "The only problem is, Mr. Horton holds the notes on those properties. How are you going to get permission from him to take some of the lumber and nails?"

"I have it all worked out Reverend, just leave that up to me."

"I don't know son, sounds like a whole bunch a foolishness to me," said daddy.

"Do you have the faith to do it, son?" asked momma.

"Yes momma, I do."

"You gonna need to put your faith to work son. Remember what da scriptures say in Hebrews 11:1 *Now faith is the substance of things hoped for, the evidence of things not seen*," she said.

"Yes, ma'am."

"Don't let nothing or nobody stand in your way son when you doing da good Lord's work. Keep da faith son, keep da faith, and everything's gonna work out fine."

"I will momma, I will."

While everyone sat on the porch talking about how hard it was going to be. Martin and my sister Cleo went for a walk in the woods. I could tell from the way they looked at each other out on Old Miller road earlier today that they were attracted to each other. I went to the edge of the woods, sat down on the dirt, and looked back at the farm, it seemed like the only one who believed we could do it was momma. Somehow she knew that this was the Lord's doing and not mine, I don't know how she knew but she did.

As the debate up on the porch continued for an hour or so, Martin and Cleo came back toward the house. Cleo was holding some wild flowers and Martin was walking with his hands behind his back. They really seemed to enjoy each others company as they walked and laughed together. As I sat on the edge of the woods looking back at the house with everyone debating about the new school and church, I was even more determined than ever, so all I could do was smile. The next morning Martin and I got up before sun up. We hitched the mule to the wagon and headed for the Horton place down Old Miller Road.

"What do you know about this Mr. Horton Jeremiah?" asked Martin.

"I know he owns most of the land around here," I said. "And I know he's a business man who's always looking for a good deal."

"I hope you know what your doing Jeremiah, because if this Mr. Horton is anything like the white folks back where I come from in Alabama, we might get shot at, just for being on his property."

"Naw, he won't shoot at us, he knows my family. My daddy sharecrops for him not to mention I used to play with his son Billy Ray when we were youngins."

"Is that right, well ya'll ain't youngins no more!"

"Just relax, and let me do all the talking."

"I hope you know what your doing Jeremiah!"

The Horton place was as beautiful as ever. That old plantation house was made of brick and it had tall white pillars in the front, and colorful flowers in the garden. Mr. Horton was out front talking with several servants when we approached, so I just drove that old mule around back.

After sitting and waiting for what seemed like hours Mr. Horton finally came out back to see what we wanted. When he came over to the wagon he immediately recognized me.

"Jeremiah, is that you?"

"Yes sir Mr. Horton. This is my friend Martin Norwood from Atlanta."

"I hear tell that you been off to college in Atlanta. How do you like the big city?"

"Well, sir, it sho is different than New Bethlehem, sir."

"I bet you learned a whole lot up at that college. What was the name of that school Jeremiah?"

"Scripture College sir!"

"Scripture College huh?"

"Yes, sir."

"What do you plan to do with yourself with all that education Jeremiah?"

"I'm going to be a school teacher, sir."

"A school teacher huh. Where do you plan to teach? You know a colored teacher can't teach in Burdonville don't you?"

"Yes sir I know, I plan on teaching in New Bethlehem."

"New Bethlehem? Where are you going to do this teaching in New Bethlehem, that old church burned down several years ago, and if I recall correctly, you are the one that burned it down, ain't that right Jeremiah?"

"Well, yes sir, I did burn it down, but it was an accident. And that's the reason I come up here Mr. Horton."

"Is that so?"

"Yes sir. I have a proposition for you Mr. Horton."

"What kind of proposition you got for me Jeremiah," he said sarcastically.

"Well sir, as everybody knows, you own just about all the land around New Bethlehem."

"That's a fact, I do."

"Well sir, I was thinking, most of the farm house's on your land are empty and boarded up. Those old barns ain't nothing but homes to raccoons, owls, and other varmints and such. Not to mention that if they was to catch on fire like that old church did, that fire might spread to the fields and destroy a whole seasons worth of cotton. That would be a whole lot of profit lost Mr. Horton.

"What are you getting at Jeremiah, I'm a busy man."

"Well sir, my friend Martin here and me would like to help you out," I said.

"We could take down those old barns and clear away the brush, and that would give you more land for raising different crops."

"Hmmm,,, that sounds interesting Jeremiah, but what do you get out of all this, I wouldn't be able to pay you very much, especially since you all educated and everything," he said sarcastically.

"You wouldn't have to pay us a penny."

"Is that right. You know I think you been out in the sun to long and it done fried your brains boy, don't know body do nothing for free, not even the colored folk."

"Well sir, we wouldn't be doing it for free."

"I done told you I wouldn't be able to pay you very much," he said. "What do you want Jeremiah?"

"All we want in return for clearing that land is the lumber from those old barns."

"Boy, I do believe you done lost your mind. Them old barns ain't good for nothing but fire wood. What are you going to do with all that wood anyway?"

"We plan to build a school and a church in New Bethlehem."

"What do you know about building anything, if I recall correctly, your daddy Matthew wouldn't let you do no type of labor when you was a youngin cause you were to scrawny?"

"Yes sir that's true, but my friend Martin here learned all about architecture in college. He's going to help me with the building."

"Is that right? I tell you what I'm gonna do Jeremiah. You and Martin go down to the old Sutton place and tear down that old shack and the barn," he said.

"After ya'll do that, I want you to clear the whole area to look like the field and if you do a good job, I'll give you half the wood."

"That's a mighty kind offer Mr. Horton, and I knows you to be a man of his word. But,,,"

"But what Jeremiah?"

"Well sir, I was hoping you might see fit to tell us right up front that we can have all the wood for clearing all that land. And,,,,"

"Spit it out boy, I don't have all day, I'm a busy man."

"I was thinking that we should get it in writing,,,, just so there wouldn't be any trouble with the decent folk of Burdonville and such. I mean we wouldn't want them to think we were stealing your property," I said nervously.

"Hmmm,,,you trying to make a deal with me Jeremiah?"

",,,,,,,umm,,yes sir,, I am!"

"This is what I'm gonna do for you. Ya'll tear down that old barn and the shack at the Sutton place, and clear the field. Then I'll let you take three quarters of the lumber. What do you think of that Jeremiah."

"That's a right friendly offer Mr. Horton. But, how's about we tear down all the barns and shacks on the Sutton place and the Brown place. Then we'll clear the ground for planting, and, we'll call the new school, Horton School, right after you?"

"Horton school?,,,,Hmmm,,,that has a nice ring to it. I like that Jeremiah. You got yourself a deal," he said with a smile.

"Will you put that on paper Mr. Horton?"

"Ain't my word good enough for ya'll?"

"Yes sir, it is. But, we just want to do things nice and legal like, so the good people of Burdonville won't misunderstand, that's all."

"Alright Jeremiah, I'll put it on paper," he said. "You drive a hard bargain Jeremiah, I see you did learn something up at that colored college."

"Thank you sir."

"When do ya'll plan to get started?"

"Right now Mr. Horton."

"Ya'll prepared to do that kind of work?"

"Yes sir!"

"What if I would have said no?"

"I never thought about that Mr. Horton," I said. "I always knew you to be fair."

"Yes sir, you show did learn something up to that colored college Jeremiah!"

We left the Horton place smiling from ear to ear. Martin couldn't believe what he just saw. "Jeremiah, I have never in my life saw a colored man negotiate with a white man the way you did," he said. "You was as smooth as a baby's bottom, where'd you learn to do that?"

"When I was a youngin, Mr. Horton used to have big parties up to his house. Well, he loved to have people tell him how important he was and how much they respected him. I just used that to our advantage, that's all."

"Well it sho did work. Did you see the look on his face when you said we were gonna name the new school after him?"

"Yep, and we're gonna do it too!"

"You plan on naming a colored school after a white man?" Are you out of your mind Jeremiah?"

"Nope, as a matter of fact, my mind ain't never been better. You don't get it do you Martin, it doesn't matter what the name of the school is, the only thing that matters is the school it self."

Martin didn't say another word about the school's name after that. The next stop after that was the old Sutton place down the road. When we got to the Sutton place we sat down at the end of the road and just stared at all the work we were about to do. I never had a second thought, but I do believe Martin had a few reservations, although he never let on. After sitting for a few minutes contemplating our next move, I drove that old mule right up to the front of the barn. When we got off the wagon we walked into the old barn. Weeds and vines had over grown the entire area and I just knew that old barn was filled with snakes and other such varmints. We rolled up our sleeves and stood there ready to work.

"Well Martin, where do we start?"

"The first thing we need to do is clear some of these vines and brush so we can see what we're doing."

"Well, let's get started," I said.

As we cleared the brush and vines, we could start to see what was left of the old barn. When we took a hammer and started to remove some of the side walls of the old barn. We must have jumped three or four feet in the air when

a few rabbits and raccoons that were living in there took off running straight into the woods. When we saw that it was only rabbits and raccoons, we started to laugh, but only for a few minutes. We worked all morning long and into the afternoon before we took a break.

But before the day was done we had completely taken that old barn apart piece by piece. We loaded as many planks on the back of the wagon as we could and made several trips down to the old church site and unloaded each load. By the end of the day we had two stacks of wood, good and bad. We managed to salvage a whole bucket of rusty nails so that we could reuse them when it came time to building. After we made the last trip and unloaded, we sat on the stack of good wood to catch our breath.

"Looks like we got more bad wood than good wood Martin!"

"Yep, seems like we do," I said. "But, we ain't finished yet. By the time we finish clearing the Sutton place and the Brown place, we should have more than enough lumber and nails to start building!"

"Maybe so Jeremiah, but,,,,,,,,"

"But what Martin?"

"We're going to need some help, I don't think we can do this alone."

"We're gonna have too, everyone around here works in the fields or in Burdonville all day, and by the time they get finished, their to tired to do anything else except eat and sleep."

We headed home tired and worn out, and like most people in New Bethlehem, we too were to tired to do anything except eat and sleep. While we were relaxing on the porch waiting for momma to call us in for supper, my brother's and sister's were just coming in from the fields. Cleo put her head down and ran into the house and grabbed a wash rag and some soap, then she ran down to the river.

I didn't realize it then, but Cleo was going to freshen up for Martin. Mean while Martin just smiled and waited for her to get back. My brother Abraham was always laughing and having fun with somebody, he walked up to the porch and he immediately started in on us.

"Well, well, well, look at baby brother. Why ya'll so tired, ya'll ain't did nothing all day sep ride around on dat wagon?" Abraham said sarcastically. "You boys ready to quit dat foolishness?"

"Foolishness, is that what you call big brother?" I asked.

"You heard me boy, ain't nothing wrong wit a school and such, but ain't no way Mr. Horton gonna let you take any wood from his property without a hefty price, but I suppose you boys found dat out today, didn't choo?"

"Well as a matter of fact big brother, we did get permission from Mr. Horton, to take all the lumber we need from the Sutton place and the Brown place," I said with pride.

"Say what, ain't no way Mr. Horton gonna do dat."

"Then how do you explain all the wood down at the old church?"

"You mean to tell me, dat Mr. Horton let ya'll take down dat old house and barn and keep da wood ta boot?"

"That's right big brother. And all we have to do is clear the land and name the school after Mr. Horton."

"Is dat right?" he said. "Ya'll gonna name a colored school after a White man?"

"It's just a name big brother, it's just a name."

"So ya'll tricked dat old cracker. I bet choo went up dare and sweet talked em, till he thought da school was his idea."

"Yeap, that's pretty much what we did."

"Boy oh boy, ya'll sho is slick, you betta hope Mr. Horton don't figure out what choo did."

"Well, it don't matter if he figure it out or not, because he gave it to us on paper!" I said with an attitude.

"He did what, he wrote it down on paper?"

"That's right, and signed his name to it. Here you want to see it?"

I pulled out that piece of paper we got from Mr. Horton and showed it to my brother. He couldn't believe what he was reading.

"Ya'll sho is slick," he said with a smile.

The next morning we picked up the lunches momma had made for us and went outside to hitch up the mule and wagon. We headed down to the Sutton place to finish demolishing the old house. When we got to the Sutton place we quickly cleared all the brush and weeds that had been growing in and around that old house for years.

We knew we were going to use the windows again so removed them first to avoid any accidents. Martin went in the old house through the front door and I went in through the back. When I got to the front room I could see Martin from down the hallway, he was standing there frozen in one spot like he had seen a ghost.

"Martin!" I said. "Martin, are you alright?"

Martin didn't answer, so I slowly walked up to him to see what he was staring at. It was human remains. I couldn't believe it, but I knew it was the remains of Mary Houston. I recognized her because of the bright pink dress torn and shattered next to her body. It was the same dress she was wearing when she disappeared. There wasn't any blood, and most of her skin was gone with the exception of a patch here and there. The braids in her hair looked as though she had just got them done. There was a pink hair bow laying next to her body, and her hands looked like claws. When I looked a little closer, I could see what appeared to be her underpants down around one leg. I suddenly got sick to my stomach, and all I could do was stand there in shock. Martin couldn't move either, he just stood there and stared at her remains.

Who could have done this I wondered. What human being could have done this to another human being, and why. There is no doubt that white people in Burdonville didn't exactly care for the colored folk in New Bethlehem but, hate to this level made me nauseous. The sight of a girl that I once knew, laying in this old decrepit building that someone once called home, was unnerving to say the least. She had a mother, daddy, brother and a sister. She wasn't just some animal that wondered off and got lost, she was loved and needed. That night we looked for her I remember thinking that she would probably show up in a day or so.

I thought that the person who might of kidnapped her would have let her go after he finished with her, but I was wrong. As I stood there that hot summer morning looking at Mary, I started to concentrate on how her hands looked like bear claws. They looked as though she had been fighting for her life. Then I remembered what I saw when all the colored men, led by Reverend Hightower went into town to get help from the sheriff, and Billy Ray had all those scratches on his neck and arms. Billy Ray claimed he got those scratches from a wild cat.

At the time I believed him because I knew he was into hurting small animals, and I thought he finally got what he deserved. But looking back in hindsight, Billy Ray most likely got those scratches from Mary Houston. I could imagine how she must have fought and struggled for her life. I don't know how she died, but by the way her body looked, she died fighting.

"Who do you think she is Jeremiah?"

"Her name was Mary Houston. She disappeared about four or five years ago."

"What do you think happened to her?"

"I don't know!" I said. "But I think we better get the Reverend."

"The Reverend, man you must be out of your mind," said Martin. "What's the Reverend going to do, this here is a matter for the law."

"Yes sir, you right Martin, only one problem."

"What's that?"

"The law might have something to do with it!"

Martin stayed with Mary's remains, while I went to get Reverend Hightower. I wasn't sure what he had in mind, but I knew he would make the right decision.

I searched all over New Bethlehem, before I finally found him asleep on the grass down by the river.

"Reverend Hightower, wake up." I shook him. "Reverend, Reverend!"

"What is it Jeremiah?" he said. "Can't you see I'm trying to get some sleep?"

"Yes sir, but you need to come with me over to the Sutton place."

"What's so important over at the Sutton place?" he said as he sat up.

"Me and Martin found,,,,,,,,,." I hesitated to answer.

"Speak up son, what did you find?"

"We found,,,,,,Mary,,,,,,,Mary Houston!"

"Dear Lord,,,,,,up at the old Sutton place?"

"Yes sir." I said. "We found her this morning."

"Help me up son. Take me over there now."

I helped the Reverend up to his feet and handed him his cane. He stumbled at first, but quickly recovered and climbed onto the wagon. The Reverend told me to drive slowly so we wouldn't raise suspicion, so I just calmly drove the wagon down Old Miller Road at a snails pace.

When we arrived at the old Sutton place, I took the Reverend into the room where we found Mary's remains. Martin was still standing in the same spot staring at her as if he couldn't move. Sweat was dripping off his forehead like a fountain. I asked him if he was ok, and he simply said "yes." The Reverend slowly approached Mary's body then kneeled down next to it. He opened up his bible and read out loud Psalms 55:4-6, *"My heart is severely pained within me, And the terrors of death have fallen upon me. Fearfulness and trembling have come upon me, And horror has overwhelmed me. So I said, "Oh, that I had wings like a dove! I would fly away and be at rest,"* he said. "Rest in peace precious one, rest in peace."

"What should we do Reverend?" I asked. "Should we call Billy Ray?"

"No Jeremiah, you know better than that."

"Then what should we do Reverend?"

As the Reverend stood there thinking he saw something shining on the side of Mary's body.

"What's this?" said the Reverend as he reached down to pick it up.

"Wait a minute Reverend, you shouldn't touch that, it looks like a piece of a gold chain," I said.

"I don't recall Mary Houston having a gold chain like that, do you Jeremiah?"

"No sir, but I know who used to have a chain just like that!"

"Who?"

"Billy Ray Horton."

"Do you know what your saying Jeremiah?" he asked. "Do you know what this means?"

"Yes sir, I do," I said. "Billy Ray had a gold pocket watch with a chain like that when we were youngins."

"Are you sure Jeremiah?"

"Yes sir, I ain't never been this sure in my whole life," I said. "That's a piece of the chain that belongs to Billy Ray's pocket watch."

"Oh dear Lord, and now he's the sheriff."

"What county is this?" I asked.

"This here is LaHaye county. Why Jeremiah?"

"What county is Burdonville in?" I asked.

"I see what your getting at, Burdonville is in Cooper county and the county line runs right through the middle of Mr. Horton's property. This here property is in LaHaye county."

"What does all that matter Jeremiah?" asked Martin.

"The town of Rosen is in LaHaye county, and they have a different sheriff, and I hear tell he's got a colored deputy working for him over there."

"Do you really think a colored deputy gonna make a difference?"

"I don't rightly know, but we should at least try. Don't you think so Reverend?"

"That would probably be our best bet Jeremiah."

Martin and I jumped on the wagon and headed for the nearby town of Rosen leaving Reverend Hightower there at the old Sutton place with Mary's body. When we got there the first thing I noticed was the fact that Rosen was much bigger than Burdonville. The colored folk and the white folk all seem to be getting along. People were in the streets talking and walking together. And I didn't see one single sign that said colored only or white only. Now that didn't mean they didn't have their fare share of problems, they just seem to tolerate one another a little better than over in Burdonville.

When we got to the middle of town we went straight to the sheriff's office. Low and behold, there he was I thought. A colored deputy, wearing his uniform as proud as you please. He was a sight to see. A dark skinned colored man with jet black eyes that felt like he could see deep into your soul when he looked at you. He walked with his thumbs in his belt and he must have stood six feet tall. He was wearing cowboy boots with spurs and he was chewing on some tobacco. When he saw us approaching he walked to the end of the steps and said, "What can I do for you boys?"

"How did you know we were here to see you?" I asked.

"Well sir, all the colored folk bring their problems to me and all the white folk take all they problems to the sheriff."

"Hmm,, well sir, my name is Jeremiah Liggons and this here is Martin Norwood. We come to see you from New Bethlehem. We have a problem down there we think you can help us with."

"New Bethlehem is in Cooper county, this here is LaHaye county."

"Yes sir we know, but, the problem we have took place in LaHaye county, at the old Sutton place, right across the county line from New Bethlehem."

"What kind of problem is it?"

"I think we should show you deputy!"

"Well give me a minute."

The deputy went inside and told the white sheriff where he was going then he came back outside and climbed on the wagon with us. We took him out to the old Sutton place where the Reverend was still there waiting. We walked through the back door and into the living room area where Mary's remains were. The deputy walked into the room and bent down over Mary's remains and looked her over. He then stood up and stared at the remains for a few seconds.

"Who is she?"

"Her name was Mary, Mary Houston," said the Reverend. "My name is Reverend Hightower."

"Please to meet you Reverend, I'm deputy Penner. Are you the one that found the body?"

"No sir, these young men were working here and they found her. They came and told me what they had found, and I came right over with them."

"So I take it that sheriff Horton doesn't know about this?"

"That's right deputy."

"That's good."

"What are you going to do deputy?"

"Well there ain't much I can do Reverend, except file a report and contact the family. Does she still have family in these parts?"

"Yes sir, her momma and daddy stay just down the road in New Bethlehem."

"How long has she been missing?" asked the deputy.

"Five or six years I suppose."

"Deputy Penner, how well do you know Billy Ray Horton?"

"Why do you ask Jeremiah?"

"I'm just curious that's all."

"I met him about a year ago when sheriff Banks died," he said. "What's on your mind Jeremiah?"

"See that gold piece of chain under Mary's right arm?"

"Yeap! What about it?"

"Sheriff Horton, used to have a gold pocket watch with a chain when we were youngins."

"What's that got to do with this?"

"Mary Houston didn't have no gold chain, in fact, don't no colored folk around New Bethlehem got no gold chains. That piece of chain is off Billy Ray's pocket watch. I'd recognize it anywhere."

"Do you have any idea what your saying Jeremiah, what are you trying to do boy, get us all lynched?"

"Can't you help deputy?" asked Martin.

"I may be a deputy, but I'm still colored. I can't go around asking no questions about a white sheriff. Wait a minute, ain't this property owned by his daddy too?"

"Yes it is."

"This is getting worse by the minute."

"Deputy Penner this poor child looks like she died a horrible death, now we don't know who did this, but her family deserves to know the truth," said the Reverend.

"Sometimes the truth is better off not told Reverend, you should know that!" he said. "Now I can take a report and take your statements, but that's about the best I can do."

"What about the piece of gold chain?"

"I'll hold on to it as evidence. Mean while, this girl needs a proper burial.'

"I'll contact the family deputy, I think it would be better if the news came from me," said the Reverend.

"I suppose your right."

Deputy Penner helped us wrap Mary's body in a old blanket we found in one of the rooms then I took Reverend Hightower and Mary's body down to the Houston farm so he could deliver the bad news about Mary to her family. We dropped Martin off at the sight of the old church and he started making a coffin out of the wood we got from the barn at the old Sutton place. The next day we had a funeral at the sight of the old church.

Martin stayed up all night and made a beautiful pine coffin and polished it until it shined. It looked like it was brand new, right out of a funeral home in Atlanta. He was truly a gifted craftsman and builder but I didn't know how I was going to talk him into staying in New Bethlehem after this. Martin was very disturbed by what had transpired. At the time I didn't know what was making Martin so upset.

He appeared to withdraw somewhat, but not when it came to Cleo. They spent more and more time together, but something just wasn't the same. I knew he had seen many dead colored folk before, and he even told me about his four friends that were lynched down in Alabama, just for smiling at a white girl. He told me that it tore him up inside but because it happened so often, it seemed like a normal way of life. Reverend Hightower's eulogy was spoken with the passion of a mad man, so full of rage, yet under control. He spoke about forgiveness and love, and at the same time he spoke of an eye for an eye. The funeral was very sad, it was as though Mary had just died that day, not five or six years earlier. I suppose in many ways, she did just die, to her family that is.

Chapter 12

The Rape

A week has passed since we had Mary's funeral. Martin and I finished tearing down the Sutton and Brown places. We cleared the land that the building once sat on and by the time we were finished, it looked as though there was never a building on that spot. It was difficult for us to work because of what we had just went through, but we knew we had to continue, despite the circumstances. Martin and my sister Cleo started spending every evening together after work, and Cleo started talking about going to college. She talked about her own hopes and dreams, something she hadn't done before she met Martin. When the time came to start building the school and church, we decided to start on the church first.

We had collected enough lumber, nails, doors and windows to make a fine church. We cleared the land next to the spot where the burnt remains of the old church were, and started building the foundation for the new church. That morning while we were working in the blazing sun, we saw little Debbie McGraw. Debbie was the daughter of Mr. Charles McGraw, the richest White man in five counties. Debbie was considered slow, because she was eighteen years old, but she had the mind of a eight year old child. Debbie often hung around New Bethlehem picking wild flowers and such out in the woods, so it wasn't unusual to see her so early in the morning.

"Hey Debbie, how are you?" I asked.

",,,,,I'm fine thank you," she said.

"What choo doin out here, picking flowers?"

",,,yes, I'm gonna take em home fo my daddy."

"That's real nice, I think yo daddy would really like that."

"What are ya'll making?" she asked

"Well, we're building a church right here and a school house over yonda."

"A church and a school?"

"Yes em."

"Can I go to school here when it's done?"

"Well,,,,,this here is a colored school Ms.Debbie," I said nervously.

"What's colored?" she asked.

"Well Ms. Debbie, I'm colored and your white and we have different schools."

"I'm white and your colored, ok, bye bye," she said. "I like ya'll school."

"Thank you Ms. Debbie, bye bye now."

"Bye bye."

Just as Ms. Debbie went off into the woods to pick wild flowers, my daddy and brothers showed up with their tools in hand.

"Hey son, hey Martin," said daddy.

"Hey daddy," I said. "What are ya'll doing?"

"Well I was thinking, don't make no since for ya'll boys to have all da fun," he said with a smile.

"Yea, as a matter of fact, ya'll been hogging up all da work round here," said Abraham.

"I don't know bout ya'll, but I comes to put in some work!" said James.

Before we knew it, they joined in and started working right along side of us. Daddy didn't look sick at all anymore, as a matter of fact, he appeared to be transformed into a new man. He had his old energy back and that pep in his step. A short while after my family arrived, Mr. Washington showed up with his tools and a lunch. He was a tall thin man, yet rugged and tough. He didn't say a word, he just watched for a few minutes then started working right along side of us. A few minutes after Mr. Washington arrived, Mr. Brown and his sons Peter and Paul showed up and joined in the work.

It wasn't long after that, that Reverend Hightower and two or three more men showed up and started working as well. As we pounded nails, and sawed lumber and such, more and more men folk arrived and started working. Martin gave instructions and they followed them to the letter, he organized the entire project. At noon time my momma and sisters showed up with baskets full of food and fresh drinking water. Martin and Cleo smiled at each other then she took a special basket she prepared just for him down to the river. I took some fried chicken and fresh made biscuits out of the basket and went and sat under an old pine tree to escape the sun.

All the men spread out in different areas to relax and have lunch. Reverend Hightower went down to the river with his fishing pole, threw out his line and laid in the grass. I don't think he was really trying to catch any fish, he just seemed to enjoy fishing. I saw Billy Ray slowly driving down Old Miller road looking at the construction site. How ironic I thought, after all these years since we burned down the old church, Billy Ray had the nerve to show up just as the new church is being built. The lunch break didn't seem to last to long, and soon Martin was saying goodbye to Cleo. He walked over to the church and started working before any of the other men finished eating their lunch, I suppose that was Martin's way of saying, it's time to get back to work. All the men responded by joining in, nobody complained, or said a word, they simply followed Martin's lead. Some of the women folk stayed behind and sang some old Negro spirituals while we worked and before to long we could see the makings of a church.

By night fall the entire building was up, the only thing we needed to do was put the windows in, the doors on and figure out a way to buy some paint. As we walked down Old Miller road headed home, we came across a homeless white family sitting on the side of the road. They were poor and desperate looking. There was a daddy, momma, two small boys that couldn't of been no older than seven or eight, and a sister about fifteen or sixteen. The children were all barefoot, hungry and dirty. The daughter's clothes were ragged and torn and it was clear she wasn't wearing any under clothes. Her breast and other private parts were exposed, but that didn't seem to matter at the time. She flirted and smiled at us, and never made an attempt to cover her self. She winked and licked her lips the way a woman does for her husband in privacy.

"Can ya'll spare some food," the daddy said with a deep country drawl.

We paused for a moment and looked around at each other. I suppose that was the first time any of us had ever seen white folks asking for food from colored folks. Suddenly everybody came up and started offering what they had left over from lunch.

"Here's some chicken and biscuits, I couldn't eat all of it. My wife made it," said Mr. Brown.

"I have some sweet potato pie left over from lunch," said Mr. Smith.

"I hope ya'll like catfish, my wife Emma fried it up in hog grease," said Mr. Brown.

"Thank you kindly, we show do appreciate this," he said.

"What's ya'll names?" I asked.

"We're da Monroe's, we're from up around Blithe county. We trying ta make it ta California, I hear tell dares work out dare," he said. "We lookin ta hop a freight train if'in we can find da rail station."

"Show nuff?" said my daddy.

"Dat's right, I hear tell dares jobs everywhere jest waitin ta be filled, and out dare, da nigger's don't take up all da good jobs from us decent white folk," he said with pride.

Suddenly all the men started walking away in disgust. Monroe just stood there with his family eating our food like they haven't had anything to eat in days. I stood there next to the Reverend while Monroe had no idea what he said.

"What's da matter?" Monroe said. "Where ya'll goin?"

"I pray that you and your family get enough to eat," said the Reverend. "Do ya'll have a place to stay the night?"

"We'll jest find some old shack somewhere I suppose."

"If you have a mind too, right down the road yonda, our new church is nearly completed, your welcome to sleep there for the night."

"Why thank you kindly boy, dats right neighborly of ya."

I couldn't imagine why even the Reverend would offer those white folks a place to lay their heads, especially after what Monroe said. The next day all the men showed up again, only this time they were there before me and Martin got there. To my surprise the Monroe family was still there. Mr. Monroe walked over to the Reverend and asked,

"How much ya'll get paid fo dis job?"

"There is no pay brother Monroe," he said. "This is the Lords work we're doing."

"Well who pays for all da supplies and such?"

"It's all a blessing from the Lord," he said with pride. "Would you like to join us and do the Lords work?"

"I would Preacher, but I got a bad back. Besides, I got's to get my family back on da road befoe sundown."

"I understand brother Monroe, and the Lord does too."

The Monroe's went and sat under some pine tree's and watched us work all morning. They never offered to lend us a hand, they just watched. Some of the men started putting in the doors and windows, and since Mr. Washington and Mr. Brown were expert carpenters they volunteered to make the congregation pews, and the Reverends podium. Everything appeared to be going just fine so Martin took a group of about eight men and went next door and started to clear the ground for the foundation of the new school.

It didn't take them long, and before we knew it they had started construction. Martin walked back and forth between the two sites continuously giving instructions and overseeing the work. The church was nearly completed by noon and it was more beautiful than the first one. There was a tall steeple with a place for a bell, and huge double entry doors for the entrance. I couldn't believe what I was seeing, this new church didn't look like the remains of an old barn and farm house. It looked as though the wood came fresh from the lumber yard in town. It was a beautiful sight and all the men stopped and looked at what they had accomplished. The Reverend called the men together to offer up a prayer to the Lord.

"Dear Lord," he prayed. "We bow down to you as your humble servants giving you all the honor, glory and praise. We thank you for giving us the strength to build this church, and most of all we thank you for your son's Martin and Jeremiah. These two fine young men allowed you to use them as vessels when you placed your vision in their hearts. This church is a testimony to your love and devotion to your people and we praise you for it in Jesus name, Amen!"

We stood up and stared at the new church in total awe. It was completed in just a few days because of all the men and their desire to be apart of something so magnificent. I never expected any of them to get involved, but I learned along time ago to trust in the Lord as my momma had always taught me. By afternoon the women folk and children had returned with lunch baskets for the men, and they all started clapping and hugging each other in disbelief.

Some fell down on their knees and thanked the Lord right on the spot. Others slowly walked around the church and touched the new building in complete amazement, while others went inside to grasp the moment. It was as though the Lord Himself had reached down and built this church on his own, it was truly awesome. During the lunch break Reverend Hightower went over and gave some food to the Monroe's. Shortly thereafter, Billy Ray drove up to the construction site in his sheriffs truck. He turned off the motor and went around to the rear of that old truck and started unloading cans of paint and brushes. There must have been a hundred gallons of white paint for the church, and a hundred gallons of red paint for the school. While he was unloading that old truck, he kept smiling at Monroe's half nude daughter as she sat under a pine tree. She must have been smitten with him as well, because she was smiling and flirting right back at him.

When he finished unloading the paint, he looked at me and smiled, got back in his old truck and drove down Old Miller road toward New Bethlehem. We didn't know what to make of it at the time, because we were all surprised at what appeared to be a very generous gift. The Reverend walked over to the paint and slowly raised his hands to the sky and yelled out, "Thank you Jesus!" I didn't know what to think myself, after all, the last time I saw Billy Ray do something kind, was when he helped me pick all those apples on Mr. Johnson's place back when we were youngins. The men folk simply went over to the school site and started working with the men that had already started over there. By the end of the day the new school was already taking shape. As all the men went their separate ways, I sat alone under a pine tree and stared at the church and school.

I was as happy as I could be, a dream was about to come true and I never doubted the good Lord for a second. That night the Monroe's asked Reverend Hightower if they could stay and rest up just one more night and he obligingly said yes. After he finished talking to them, Reverend Hightower grabbed his fishing pole and went down to the river as he did just about every night to pray and fish I suppose. When I got up to leave after sitting there for an hour or so, I heard a loud eerie scream coming from the woods behind the new school. *"Ignore it and go home*," I heard the Angel say, but I couldn't, so I ran as fast as I could in the direction of the scream. When I arrived I didn't see anything. I looked everywhere for all of ten or fifteen minutes, but I didn't see anything or anyone. Just as I was about to leave, I found Monroe's daughter laying on the grass. She was completely naked, her clothes had been torn off her body, and she wasn't moving. She had a piece of rag tied around her eyes, and her hands were tied behind her back. I kneeled down next to her and shook her shoulder trying to wake her up, but she didn't move.

At that moment I realized that the man who had been attacking and raping colored girls was back and now he had just raped a white girl. I nervously stood up and felt something wet on my hands, when I took a closer look, I saw that it was blood. Then suddenly I could hear her father calling for her, and before I knew it he was right behind me. "*I know your afraid, but don't run now, they'll think you did this,*" said the Angel. But fearing for my life, I took off running into the woods toward the river anyway. I know I didn't do anything wrong, but I didn't want to get blamed for something as bad as this. I ran and hid deep in the woods all the while fighting off mosquitoes that seem to be attracted to my open wounds. Then the fog started to roll in like a wool blanket, blocking out the moonlight and casting darkness upon me.

It was so dark I couldn't see my hand in front of my face, but that was the least of my worries because I was surrounded by water moccasin's. I climbed up a tree hoping to escape the night creatures that call the woods their home. The night was long and cold and I didn't sleep a wink. As the sun began to rise and the fog started to fade, it wasn't long after that that I could hear hound dogs barking in the distance. I knew they were coming for me and that death was imminent. I climbed down that tree and started to run. I tried to throw them off my trail by tearing up pieces of my shirt and scattering them in different areas. I put a couple of rags on some drift wood and put it in the river hoping the hounds would catch that scent and head down river while I went up river, but it didn't work, those dogs were right on my trail.

I felt like a runaway slave, soaked to the bone, scared, alone and innocent, but so were they and none of that stopped those slave catchers from lynching beating and killing those runaways. I thought about climbing another tree but I didn't have the strength. I just kept moving as fast as I could. I was covered in mud and leaves looking every bit a guilty monster. My blood continued to flow from all the scratches and cuts made by the branches while I was running in the night. After a while I couldn't take another step, I was to exhausted to move so I just fell down in the mud and collapsed. Soon those hound dogs were all around me and I could hear white men yelling as they got closer.

"Thar he is, get dat nigger!" someone shouted.

"Get em fo he gets away!" said another.

"Hang em, hang em," they all yelled. "Get a rope!"

"We'll sho ya what we do ta nigger's who puts his hands on a white girl!"

That lynch mob grabbed me and put a rope around my neck and threw the other end up over a branch. I started to pray out loud.

"PLEASE LORD, DON'T LET THEM LYNCH ME," I prayed.

"Ain't no sense in you calling on da good Lord boy, ain't nothing gonna save yo black ass now, so you might as well shut up!" a white man shouted.

"PLEASE LORD, HELP ME," I shouted.

"I said shut up," he yelled as he struck me with his fist. "Don't you understand English boy?"

They covered my mouth with a piece of my shirt then tied my hands behind my back and hoisted me up to my feet. They took turns beating me with the but of their shot guns and fist. When they were done someone yelled out, "string em up." And before I knew it I was swinging by my neck. As I swung back and forth by my neck gasping for air, I saw a bright light directly in front of me, and the Angel appeared in that light and said, *"The Lord told you He would never leave you nor forsake you."* Then I heard a shotgun blast and the branch break then I fell to my knees then on my face. "Ain't nobody gettin hung today," a voice said. I recognized the voice, it was Billy Ray.

"Now what da hell you boys thank you doin?" he said. "Dis here is a matter fo da law, take dat rag out a his mouth and untie em!"

"Damn it Billy Ray, that nigger raped a white girl," said Homer"Homer, were you there?" he said. "Was any of ya'll there, I didn't thank so, now do what I said befoe I forget were neighbors!"

"But dat gals daddy was there, he seen da whole thang, tell em Monroe," said Homer as he untied me.

Just then Monroe nervously stepped forward staring at me as if I were guilty. "Well sir, I heard my daughter screamin and I went a lookin for her, and I seen dat nigger standing over her, when he seen me he took off into da woods like a bat out a hell. My baby girl was all beat up and bleeding and such, I could tell dat nigger had his way wit her," he said.

"You ain't from round here are you?" asked Billy Ray.

"No sir, me and my family jest passing through on our way ta California."

"Is that right?" asked Billy Ray. "What happened Jeremiah?"

I could hardly breath and I had blood all over my face from the beating I took, but I managed to get out a few words.

"I,,,,, ain't,,,,,, hurt nobody, Billy Ray!"

"If dats true, you ain't got nothing ta worry bout. Come on, get up on yo feet, I'm taking you in ta Burdonville."

"Ahh,, come on Billy Ray, dat old Judge Parker ain't gonna do nothing sep put dat boy in jail," said Homer. "We can save da county money if we strang em up right here and now."

"I done told choo once Homer, and da rest of ya'll listen up, ain't nobody gettin hung, not today anyway," said Billy Ray. "Now help em up, ya'll damn near killed em, now ya'll carry em out da woods and put em in my truck."

Those white men were mad as could be but they listened to Billy Ray and carried me out of the woods and put me in the back of Billy Ray's truck. He took me to Burdonville and put me in jail with several other colored boys that were in jail for some minor offenses like trespassing, disorderly conduct and for being drunk in public. The inside of that jail was filthy. It smelled like rotting fish and there were horse flies, gnats and mosquitoes every where.

Rats and roaches were everywhere and there was only one bed, even though there were five or six of us in there. Those boys let me have the bed since I was all beat up and such. Billy Ray called old doc Smith to come over and take a look at me, but he was too drunk. So Billy Ray called the veterinarian and he finally showed up after several hours. He examined me right in the middle of that pig sty Billy Ray called a jail. The vet cleaned up my wounds and bruises just like I was a beat up mule. I remember thinking that at least a mule was treated like a mule. Before the vet left the cell some of them colored boys asked him to take a look at their cuts and scrapes but he said he was running late for another appointment, so he left. One colored boy who couldn't of been a day over sixteen just sat in the corner and cried. When I asked some of the others what was wrong with him, they said,

"He's jest scared he might be next," said one prisoner.

"Next for what," I asked.

"Every night the sheriff open up the cell and the white men come and take one of us out," he said.

"Where do they take em," I asked.

"Man we don't know, but one thang we do know, da ones dey takes out, don't never come back," said another prisoner.

Later that afternoon my daddy, brothers and Martin came with Reverend Hightower to see me in the jail. I could hear daddy talking with Billy Ray in the front office, but I couldn't quite make out their conversation, but after they finished talking Billy Ray let my daddy come back to the cell alone.

"Ahh, Jeremiah, your daddy's here ta see ya!"

"Daddy, I didn't do what they said I did," I cried.

"I know son, I know," he said. "I don't know how I'm gonna do it, but so help me God I'll find a way to get choo out a dis cage.

"Daddy, is that white gal dead?"

"No, she's alive. Do you remember Mrs. Jackson, the widow lady over on Tanglewood street?"

"Yes sir, the white lady with the big yellow house?"

"Well, she done took in da whole Monroe family, and the doctor over there tending to that child right now," he said. "Sister Burgess works in her house and she over heard the doctor saying she gonna be jest fine."

"Thank God, thank God," I cried. "Now she can tell her daddy and Billy Ray it wasn't me that hurt her!"

"Dat's my hope son, dat's my hope!"

As my daddy and I talked he had tears in his eyes. He looked weary and worn and I could see father time catching up with him, and there wasn't a thing in the world I could do about it. My daddy's life was spent taking care of momma and all of us youngins. He never asked for anything in return except obedience, respect, and hard work. That wasn't much to ask of your family in return, considering how much he gave. As I stood there looking at my daddy, I felt that if I didn't get out of this mess soon, I might not ever see my daddy again. Billy Ray came to the cell where me and my daddy were talking.

"Hey Jeremiah!"

"Hey Billy Ray!"

"I got some bad news for ya," he said. "Dat Monroe gal, says it was a colored man that raped her."

"How does she know who it was? When I found her her eyes were covered with a rag and her hands were tied," I cried.

"Jeremiah,,,she said you asked her if she liked colored men! I have to keep you in jail,,,,,,and there's gonna be a trial,,,,,for rape!"

"Billy Ray,,,you know me, you know I would never even look at a white gal," I pleaded.

"I know Jeremiah,,,but she says it was a colored man and you were the only colored man anywhere near her, besides,,,,why did you run if you was innocent?"

"Have you forgotten Billy Ray?"

"Forgotten? Forgotten what?"

"I'm a colored man in a white man's world, what would you have done if you were me Billy Ray?" I pleaded. "What chance does a colored man have when a white gal say he raped her?"

"I'll do all I can Jeremiah,,,, but I can't make no promises," said Billy Ray.

Billy Ray just stood there and appeared to be really concerned. He looked sad, just like the time he found me working on Mr. Johnson's place picken apples because of something he did. For the first time since I was a child, I was afraid, really afraid.

Chapter 13

New Lessons

Shortly after my daddy and Billy Ray left the cell, all the colored men in that jail cell with me immediately started to attack me verbally. They gathered around in an attempt to intimidate me with their hostility and anger.

"What do you know bout pain and suffering boy, you look like you one dem uppity Negroes from Atlanta?" said an old colored man.

"You don't know nothing bout no struggles boy," said another.

"Boy, you don't even know who you is, talkin all friendly wit da sheriff," said another.

"I bet choo thank you white boy, don't choo?" said another.

"What choo know bout being colored boy?" said still another.

The anger and frustration I felt was overwhelming and I couldn't contain myself any longer, so I unleashed as much knowledge as I could on them. "I'll tell you what I know and who I am, and if you pay close attention I'll tell you who you are as well," I said angrily. "Throughout the ages and without apology my people have been the object of persecution, ridicule and hate. We were kidnapped from our home never to see it again. We left behind a heritage, culture, religion and a way of life, all of which would take hundreds of years to recapture. We were chained together in ways an animal couldn't bare, and forced to lie down one on top of another, crammed into coffin like quarters beneath the deck of the slave ship. The dead appear to have life, as their bodies are tossed back and forth, seemingly in rhythm with the ships movement, all the while still shackled next to the living.

The stench of human waste and rotting flesh fill the air. The moans and groans of those in pain is drowned out by the loud and ferocious sound of the ocean, as it pounds mercilessly against the hull of the ship, tossing it about as if it too wanted to own it's cargo. Unable to stand or even sit up, each warrior had no choice but to watch helplessly as his wife, mother, daughter or sister was taken away to be beaten and raped. The iron shackles ripped at our beautiful black & brown flesh until it became a bloody mess. The nights were cold and wet as each man woman and child slept and dreamed of home, only to wake up in hell's reality.

"What have we have done to deserve this treatment?" a Princess cried out. "Do not fear," said a young African King. "God will protect us." "Where do they come from and what are they going to do with us, your majesty?" said others. "We must rise up and fight," yelled the warriors. When we were taken aboard that ship our numbers were nearly five hundred, but when we arrived in the land of the free, we numbered less than half.

They moved us out of the dark belly of the slave ship into the blinding bright sun. We were barely able to move, close to death, yet clinging to life. The blood of our ancestors would soon spill to the ground, and change the color of time, forever. They lined us up according to age and gender, then began to inspect our teeth, buttocks, vagina's and penis's. "This buck is powerfully built, he's probably stronger than an ox," said a pale skinned man. "Look at this one, she's going to give me a great deal of pleasure, as well as make me some slave babies," another said laughingly. The sound of a whip crackled over and over again as the strange pale men and women moved cautiously through the maze of black & brown shackled men, women and children.

They suddenly stop in front of one peculiar African, he doesn't seem to fear them as the others do. With his head held high he stares them down without blinking. The contempt and anger he feels is seen in his eyes. Suddenly, the first of many slashes with the whip cut through the air landing on his back, slicing into his body like melted butter. "I'll teach you what happens when you look a white man in the eye, nigger," said a voice from behind.

He struggled to free himself, but that young African King was beaten until he died. He was an example of what was to come if any others were so strong or proud. Soon we were working on plantations, picking cotton, peaches, tobacco, sweet potatoes or peanuts. We were carpenters, black smiths, drivers, maids, mammies, butlers and concubines. Our first families were no more, an our new one would soon follow. Our babies were snatched right out of our arms and sold to the highest bidder.

Two or three hundred years have passed and we were set free. I wonder how many millions of my people have been murdered during that time, I suppose an astronomical amount. Who was ever brought to justice for the worlds most notorious, brutal, sadistic, cruel and inhumane crimes against humanity, perpetrated by evil? No one, that's who! In school I was told Abe Lincoln set our people free. At home, I was told our Lord and Savior Jesus Christ delivered us from bondage and set us free. Some of us headed north to escape the memory of the past and attempt to start a new life.

This happiness was short lived and the new era of slavery was just beginning. The shackles were gone only to be replaced by drugs and alcohol. Despite the planned attempt to destroy my people, we're over coming tremendous obstacles everyday. We have colored College graduates, Doctor's, Lawyers, Inventors, Politicians, Entertainers, Engineers, Artists, CEOs, Entrepreneurs, Scientist, Military servicemen, Teachers and Preachers. We raised our families and obeyed all the laws and yet we are still outcast in a land that no longer needs, nor wants us. We built this land from the ground up, each layer of cement is soaked in our peoples blood, and the roots of every plant is nourished with our peoples sweat and tears.

We continue to be victimized in a society that labels it's money, "In God We Trust." The body of a colored man swinging from a tree with a wooden cross burning in the background was a common sight after slavery. Seems like only yesterday I heard about a colored man who was beaten and dragged behind a horse until his head and arms were severed and left on the side of a dark country road.

Oh yea, it was only yesterday and slavery has been over for almost eighty years. It seems like the color of my skin still invokes anger, contempt and hatred. Once in a while time appears to stand still and we live our lives in a constant battle not for supremacy, but for survival. And just like my God set us free from slavery, He will also set us free from racism, hatred, violence, poverty, envy and strife. Now, if you don't think I know who, what and where I am, your all a bunch of fools," I said with an attitude. I felt like a warrior that day, and my wounds were my battle scars, and my knowledge was my truth.

Those colored men stood there looking at me in amazement. It occurred to me that they probably never heard a colored man speak with such knowledge and passion before and they didn't know how to respond. They all slowly walked away except one.

"Where you learn all dat?" asked a young colored boy.

"College!" I said with pride.

"You been to college?" he asked.

"Yes sir, a colored college up in Atlanta."

"You mean ta tell me, dat there's a colored college in Atlanta?"

"Yes sir!"

"I ain't never been pass da third grade, how you get in a colored college?"

"My momma cleaned white folks houses and cooks their meals, and my daddy and brothers share crops for Mr. Horton. They saved up the money to send me, and I worked two jobs when I got there."

"Sho nuff?"

"That's right!" I said. "You can do it too if you have a mind to."

"I don't know bout dat!"

"Look here,,,,,what's your name?"

"Louis."

"Louis, a colored man ain't got no choice but to get educated, otherwise the white man gonna always have you working for him."

"The white man ain't gonna let me get no education, I got's ta help my daddy round da farm, ain't no time fo no education."

"Can you read Louis?"

"I can't read or write to good."

"I tell you what, when you get out of here, I'll give you some books that helped me when I was learning, and I'll teach you how to read and write, how does that sound?"

"Dat sounds good, but,,,,ain't dey gonna hang you?" he said with sadness.

",,,,,,,,,,,I,,,,,,,I,,hope not Louis,,,I hope not."

"What about in here, can you teaches me in here, Teacher?" he asked.

I paused for a moment, not because I didn't have the answer, but because I didn't plan on being in jail much longer. The reality of the matter was, I was a colored man accused of raping a white girl, now if the law don't kill me, then them good folks of Burdonville show will.

"I suppose I could teach you to read and write right here!"

"Wow!" he yelled. "I come to jail for trespassing on white folks land, and I gonna gets a education, in jail. Now don't dat beet all?"

"Well, don't get to excited yet. I don't know if the sheriff will let me have my books in here."

"Well why not, I mean you and dat sheriff act like you old friends and such, I mean you callin em by his first name and all."

"I knew him along time ago Louis, back when we was youngins."

"Den what's da matter Teacher?"

",,,,,We ain't youngins no more!"

Maybe Billy Ray would remember all the times I got in trouble for something he did and be kind enough to let me teach Louis to read, I thought. Friendship is a funny thing, I don't know that Billy Ray and I are friends, but we weren't exactly enemies either. The next day I could hear the sound of keys jingling and hitting medal, then the sudden crash of the cell doors opening.

"Wake up Jeremiah," I heard a voice say. "Wake up!"

I pretended to be sleep, because I didn't know what was about to happen. I peeked out of the corner of my eyes, and everyone in that cell was looking as though they had seen a ghost. They stared at me with fear and trembling in their eyes, then I remembered what they told me the day before about Billy Ray opening the cell to let some white man come in and take colored men out. I remembered that they also told me that those men disappeared, never to be seen again.

"I said wake up Jeremiah," the voice demanded. "Wake up!"

"Ain't no since pretending like ya sleep, dey gonna takes you anyhow," said a colored man.

"You best go wit da sheriff Jeremiah, ain't nothing you can do bout it!" said another.

"All da book learnin in da world cain't save ya now," said another. "Gone now, fo he takes one of us in yo place."

I slowly opened my eyes and sat up. My wounds had hardened and the blood was dry, but the pain had not gone away. I looked around the cell for Louis, and I saw him cowering in the corner of the cell shaking like a scared rabbit. I stood up and walked over to the door and stood right in front of Billy Ray. I felt that if I was going to die, I'd die with some dignity, not cowering and screaming for my life. He took me by the arm and moved me into the hall, then closed the door behind him.

Then he pointed down the hall at a huge wooden door, and told me to go in that direction, so I did. When I got to the door, he opened it and we went inside. On the other side of that door was a long hallway with more jail cells. To my surprise there were more colored men down that hall. There must have been eight or ten of them at least. As it turns out, all he wanted to do was move me out of that crowded cell and put me in one by myself down the hall.

"Billy Ray!"

"Stop calling me Billy Ray, Jeremiah, it's sheriff Horton!" he said emphatically.

"Sheriff Horton?" I said. "You seem to be forgetting allot these days Billy Ray," I said. "Sheriff Horton sounds official and all, but I know you, I knew you when you was peaking in colored gals windows at night, and I was there when you,,,,,,,,,"

"Alright," he said abruptly. "But don't be callin me by my first name in front of da prisoners," he said in a whisper.

"I don't mean no disrespect Billy Ray, but I just don't think I got much time for formalities and such," I said. "Billy Ray, I need a favor if you can."

"What is it?"

"That young colored boy in the other cell."

"What about em?'

"Can you move him down here in this cell with me?"

"Why would I do dat Jeremiah?"

"Because I'm asking Billy Ray," I said. "He wants to learn to read and write."

"And I suppose you gonna teach em?"

"I am a teacher Billy Ray."

'Dat's right, you been up to Atlanta at some colored college," he said. "You know, folks round here always did wonder where yo daddy get dat kinda money to send you to college."

"You know good and well where my daddy got that money Billy Ray," I said with anger.

"I don't know, no such thang Jeremiah!" he said. "People round here can't feed dey families with da depression and all, but yo daddy sends you to college?"

"What are you trying to say Billy Ray?"

"I'm jest sayin, folks round here don't like uppity nigger's, dats all."

"Is that what I am to you Billy Ray, an uppity nigger?"

"Well,,,,you are uppity," he said sarcastically.

"Billy Ray,,,,,,will you please move that boy in here with me, so I can help him?"

"You don't even sound like a nigger no more, you sound like dem white folks up north," he said. "How dey teach you dat?"

"Teach me what?"

"To sound like a white man," he said jealously.

"How am I suppose to sound Billy Ray?" I said. "Would you be happier if I spoke wit dat twang and drawl, like I used too?"

"You makin fun a me Jeremiah?" he said. "Don't forget, I am da sheriff."

"How can I forget that Billy Ray? You are wearing the sheriff's badge."

"Dat's right!"

I paused for a moment and thought about something my momma once told me. She said it is easier to catch a bear with honey than with vinegar. So with that in mind, I changed my tone and dialect in order to appease Billy Ray so that he would allow me the opportunity to teach Louis to read and write.

"Billy Ray, I mean sheriff Horton, do ya thank it would be possible ta move dat young colored boy into dis cell so I can teach em ta read and write?"

"Well, well, well,,now you sound like a nigger from round here again Jeremiah," he said with a smile. "I don't see why not, after all I am da sheriff."

"Thank ya kindly,,,,sheriff Horton," I said. "One more thang sheriff Horton, would you be so kind as to get me my books, some paper and a pencil from my daddy, sa?"

"Well, as da sheriff I suppose I could do that for ya Jeremiah!"

"Thank ya sheriff."

"Hey Jeremiah don't forget who you are when you go before Judge Parker, he ain't as friendly as me, some say he's down right nasty when it comes to colored boys raping white girls."

Billy Ray left that cell with a big smile on his face. A short while later he came back with Louis and put him in my cell. Billy Ray handed me my books, some paper and a pencil to write with. He was smiling like he knew something I didn't know, and I suppose he did. After all, he was the sheriff, at least that's what he kept telling me. Several weeks passed, and Louis was learning faster than I could have ever imagined. He didn't seem to care anymore that he was in jail, he just wanted to learn.

I was so caught up in teaching Louis that I hadn't realized that my momma and daddy hadn't been to see me since I first got locked up. Those thoughts started to eat away at me and I started getting lonely and afraid all over again. Several more weeks went by before a lawyer came in and to see me. He was a tall slender white man with gray hair. He was an unusual sight, because he had the face of a man in his twenties yet his gray hair gave the impression that he was much older. He appeared to be nervous and very apprehensive. His suit looked as though it belonged to his great granddaddy, it was worn out with several small holes in the sleeve.

"Jeremiah Liggons?" he said nervously.

"I'm Jeremiah Liggons."

"I'm your court appointed lawyer. My name is Alexander Billingsworth III," he said with an English accent. I plan to do all I can to see to it that you get a fair trial and if all goes well you won't have to go to a prison to far for your family to visit."

"Excuse me Mr. Billingsworth, but did you say something about prison?"

"Well,,,,yes,,,is there a problem Jeremiah?"

"You damn right there's a problem, I didn't do it," I said with anger.

"Oh,,,,that does pose a bit of a problem," he said. "I was under the impression that you were caught in the act of violating young Jessica Monroe," he said surprisingly.

"That's not the truth, I never ever put my hands on that gal! I found her that's all."

"But the sheriff's report says that young Jessica Monroe named you as the perpetrator."

"I don't care what she says, I didn't do it."

"You watch your tone with me Jeremiah," he said nervously. "I'm not some local hick that you can intimidate. I'm an educated man, and I'm here to help you."

"If your here to help me, then shouldn't you get to the truth?" I said. "Someone else hurt that gal, and it wasn't me. Somebody been raping colored gals down in New Bethlehem for years, maybe he's the one that raped Jessica Monroe!"

"Make no mistake Jeremiah, I will do all I can to help you," he said. "And I assure you, it would be much easier on your family if you just admit your crime, and not try and pass it off on some fictitious assailant."

"You listen to me, I did not touch that gal. I found her after someone else,,,,,,,"

"Jeremiah, when I was in law school at Princeton, one of my professors told us about the colored men here in the south. He told us how they desire white women, and how they will not take no for an answer," he said. "Is that what really happened Jeremiah, she said no?"

"I'm only going to tell you this one more time Alexander, I did not touch that white gal and I don't appreciate your condescending, pampas, attitude. I don't know very much about Princeton, but in the rest of America a man is presumed innocent until proven guilty, even a colored man!"

"Well now,,,,,as I said,,,, I shall do all I can to help you,,,,,under the circumstances," he said as he wiped the sweat from his forehead.

When Billingsworth left the jail, he walked at a brisk pace as if he had somewhere to go, and he was in a hurry to get there. Louis sat in awe and listened to the whole conversation.

"Dey must a really hit choo hard in yo head, teacher."

"Why do you say that, Louis?"

"Where I come from, talkin like dat to a white man will get you hung fo sho."

"Don't be mistaken Louis, it's the same way around here, I just don't see that I have a choice anymore. Remember, I'm fighting for my life."

"But what if'in dey hang ya befoe ya can get in da fight, what choo gonna do den?"

"I'll hold my head up high, put my shoulders back and die like a man, on my own two feet," I said. "Do you know why I would do that Louis?"

"No sa! Why?"

"Because I'm innocent, and innocent men don't have anything to be afraid of."

Chapter 14

The Trial

The day had finally come for me to go to trial. Billy Ray and his new deputy came to take me out of the cell. They were holding shot guns and carrying shackles.

"What are the shotguns for sheriff," I asked.

"Your protection Jeremiah," he said. "There's a whole bunch a people out there dat wants ta hang you fo what choo did. And I aim ta make sho it don't happen."

"Are you prepared to shoot a white man to protect me sheriff?"

",,,,,,,I'm prepared to do da right thang."

"I hope you know what your doing."

They shackled me from head to toe. I could barely walk and they had to hold my arms to help me, and their shotguns at the same time. As we walked down the hall of the jail, all of the colored prisoners stood by the bars of their cell and stared at me with sadness in their eyes. I felt as though I was a condemned man on my way to be executed. We left the jail and went out through the side door to avoid the white mob that had gathered out front, but one of the young white boys saw us and shouted,

"Dare dey is!"

"Get in da truck Jeremiah," Billy Ray shouted.

While the deputy helped me get into the truck, Billy Ray walked up to the white mob and pointed his shotgun in the air as they approached. They had ropes, guns, and pitchforks.

"Ya'll go home now," said Billy Ray.

"We ain't goin nowhere till dat nigger get what's comin to em,' a white man shouted.

"He's on his way to da court house fo a trial, and I aim ta get em there in one piece."

"What bout three or four pieces Billy Ray?' said Homer. "All you got ta tell judge Parker is, you got hit from behind, and you don't know what happened after dat."

"Yea Billy Ray, what choo care fo anyway, he ain't nothing but a nigger rapist," shouted Clyde.

"Now I'm only gonna say this one mo time, da first one a ya'll try an take my prisoner, I'm gonna shoot em dead, and dat goes fo you Homer, and you Clyde."

The mob stood there for a moment and Billy Ray walked backwards, still pointing his shotgun at the crowd and slowly got into the truck with me and the deputy. He drove right through the crowd real easy like and they all stepped aside and watched us drive by. Some of those white folks went and got on there horses and some got in there trucks and cars and followed us to the court house at the other end of town. Judge Parker was an old southerner with deep roots in the south and the Confederacy. His beard was as white as cotton, with white skin to match. He carried a bible everywhere he went, even though nobody ever recalled seeing him open it, let alone read from it. He wore an old confederate hat with gold tassels hanging from it, and the confederate flag was hanging in his court room.

We entered the court through the side door and they sat me down shackles and all at a desk next to my so called lawyer, Alexander Billingsworth. As I looked around the court room, I saw most of the colored folks from New Bethlehem including my family standing outside looking in through the windows. I turned around to look at the spectators and I saw young Jessica Monroe sitting in the front row. She was dressed in a beautiful dress, and her momma and daddy were dressed in fine new clothes as well, I could hardly recognize them. She wasn't smiling or flirting the way she did with the colored men that first day we saw them on Old Miller road and she never looked at Billy Ray the way she did back at the new church.

She looked as pure and innocent as could be, just like one of them high society white gals from Atlanta. Suddenly I heard a loud voice yelling in the court room. "Order in the court. All rise, the honorable Judge Parker presiding." Everyone stood up as Judge Parker entered the court and sat down at the bench. "You may be seated and come to order," said the court officer. As everyone in the court room sat down a hush fell over the court room like a funeral.

Nobody was saying a word, as we all watched Judge Parker flip through some papers and occasionally take a sip of brandy, provided by the court officer. Then, in a deep southern drawl Judge Parker said, "How does your client plead Mr. Billingsworth?" Billingsworth stood up and adjusted his coat and tie, then cleared his throat. ",,,,,,,,,,Not,,,,,,guilty your honor!" At that moment the entire court room erupted in disbelief. "Quiet in the court room, quiet in the court room," shouted the court officer.

The spectators slowly quieted down, then Judge Parker spoke. "The next disruption like that and I'll clear the entire court room, and you all will have to listen from outside, do I make myself perfectly clear. This is a court of law, not a baseball game, and you will all conduct yourselves accordingly." After that outburst in the court room, Billingsworth was even more nervous than he was before and it could be seen in his eyes.

He looked around the court room nervously wiping the sweat from his forehead and continuously clearing his throat. I remember thinking how strange it was to have a white lawyer representing me in a trial, where I was accused of raping a white girl, and the lawyer was more nervous than I was.

That sure was strange, especially because I was the one on trial, and it was my neck on the line, not his.

"Did you say not guilty, Mr. Billingsworth?" asked Judge Parker.

",,,,,,Yes,,sir,,,not guilty!"

"I see. The evidence seems to be overwhelming, are you quite sure your client wants to plead not guilty?"

",,,,,I've discussed this matter with my client,,,,and he insist on pleading not guilty,,,your honor."

"If that's the case, I am bound by law to hold a trial. The court will now recess for one hour while I select a jury. I want all able bodied men to stay in the court room, and the rest of you please go outside. Sheriff, take the prisoner back to the jail, I'll call for you when we are ready to begin."

"Yes sir," said Billy Ray.

Billy Ray took me back to the jail and put me in my cell and we waited about two, maybe three hours before the judge sent word for us to return to the court house. When we arrived back to the court house, I wasn't surprised to see the jury had already been selected, and they were some of the same white men that tried to lynch me down in the woods several weeks before. Now I knew I was gonna hang for sure. Those white men couldn't hang me illegally the first time, now they were gonna get a second chance, only this time they were going to use the law.

"Order in the court. All rise, the honorable Judge Parker presiding." Everyone stood up as Judge Parker entered the court and sat down at the bench. "You may be seated and come to order," said the court officer.

"Mr. Billingsworth, have you by any chance been able to convince your client to change his plea to guilty?" asked the Judge. Billingsworth stood up and very nervously cleared his throat.

"No your honor, my client wishes for his original plea of not guilty to stand."

"Very well then. Mr. Morgan, proceed with your opening statement."

Mr. Morgan stood up to speak, he was a local prosecutor, a short white man with a bald head. He wore silver framed glass's that were very thick and he spoke very slow and to the point.

"Your honor, gentlemen of the jury. This is a simple case. The state will prove beyond a reasonable doubt that the defendant, Jeremiah Liggons watched, stalked, and viciously raped Miss. Jessica Monroe, this young, vulnerable, sweet, innocent white girl. She was as pure as the driven snow, until this nigger put his filthy hands on her," he shouted.

"Your honor I object!"

"You object to what Mr. Billingsworth?"

"The use of the word nigger, it's prejudicial and degrading, my client's name is Jeremiah Liggons!"

The people in the court room immediately started mumbling to one another. "Quiet in the court room, quiet in the court room," shouted the court officer. Judge Parker paused for a moment and stared at Billingsworth as if he didn't like him very much.

"Where are you from Mr. Billingsworth?" asked Judge Parker.

"I'm from England, your honor."

"Where did you go to law school?"

"I attended Princeton School of law, your honor."

"That's a fine school Mr. Billingsworth, and no doubt you received a fine education there, however, I need to remind you that this is not the North, it is the South. We have our own way of doing things around here."

"I understand that your honor but my client should not be subjected to name calling by the prosecutor!"

"Mr. Billingsworth, you don't want to anger the court, it wouldn't be good for your,,,,,,,client now would it?"

Billingsworth looked around the court room and nervously sat down. I remember thinking that I was wrong about him, he was going to fight for me, even if it meant he would probably never work in this town or any other town in the South again.

"Mr. Morgan, you may finish your opening statement."

"As I was saying before I was interrupted by my esteemed adversary. The state will prove beyond a shadow of doubt that Jeremiah Liggons is guilty as charged and should be sent to prison for the rest of his natural life."

"Your opening statements Mr. Billingsworth."

"Your Honor, my client is innocent of all charges, he was simply coming to the aide of Miss. Monroe because he heard her screaming in the woods. Upon my clients arrival, the true perpetrator had fled the scene. My client is only guilty of being in the wrong place at the wrong time, and according to my esteemed adversary Mr. Morgan, he's also guilty because of the color of his skin!"

"Your honor is that necessary?" asked Mr. Morgan.

"Absolutely not. Mr. Billingsworth, one more remark like that and you will find yourself in contempt of this court, and I'll have you thrown in jail right next to your client. Do I make myself perfectly clear sir?"

"Yes your Honor, I apologize to the court."

Mr. Morgan sat at his table and smiled and most of the men in the jury thought it was pretty funny also. At first I wasn't sure if Billingsworth was helping my case or making it worse, but at least I felt like I had a fighting chance.

"Now do you have any further opening remarks?" asked the Judge.

"No your Honor."

"Good, then let's get started, Mr. Morgan you may begin."

"I'd like to call my fist witness, the widow Jackson."

The widow Jackson was dressed in a beautiful beige dress with all kinds of lace and her hat matched perfectly. She was wearing real pearls around her neck and she was holding a small fan as she walked to the witness stand.

"Place your left hand on the bible and raise your right hand mam," said the court officer. "Do you swear to tell the whole truth and nothing but the truth so help you God?"

"I do!"

"You may be seated."

"Ms. Jackson, how are you ma'am?" asked Mr. Monroe.

"I'm just fine, thank you for asking."

"Ms. Jackson, will you tell the court exactly what you saw the night Miss. Monroe came to your home?"

"Well sir, she was badly beaten and bruised. She was covered in blood from head to toe and,,,,,,."

"And what Ms. Jackson?"

"And I could see that she had been,,,,,,."

"Please go on Ms. Jackson, I realize this is very uncomfortable for you, but please go on."

"I could see that she had been,,,,,,violated."

"Violated?"

"Yes sir, by that young man right over there, Jeremiah Liggons."

"Your Honor I object, the witness was not present at the time of the alleged assault!" said Billingsworth.

"Sustained. Ms. Jackson, please refrain from voicing your personal opinion."

"I'm sorry Judge."

"What was Miss. Monroe wearing when they brought her to your house?"

"Not much of anything, her clothes were just bloody rags."

"Is that right, bloody rags you say?"

Mr. Morgan picked up a brown paper bag, then walked over to the jury, and in the most dramatic fashion, reached inside that bag and pulled out some bloody clothes, and held them up for the entire court room to see.

"This is evidence number one. These torn. bloody rags are all that is left of Miss. Jessica Monroe's dress. This is all the defendant left when he brutally and savagely raped and beat this poor white girl. If you take a look at her, you can see that she has healed, but not completely. Some of the scars are still visible from her attack."

"Do you have anymore questions for this witness?"

"No sir."

"Mr. Billingsworth, you may cross examine this witness, and be advised, Ms. Jackson is a Southern Lady, show some respect," said the Judge.

"Ms. Jackson, are you a medical doctor?"

",,,Of course not!"

"Have you had any medical training?"

"No I have not, and for your information, my husband was the late Coronal Jackson!"

"That's wonderful. So you don't know anything about medical procedures and examinations do you Ms. Jackson?"

"No, I do not, but what does this have to do with this case?"

"I'm glad you asked that Ms. Jackson and that leads to my next question. If you don't have any medical training or any back round in medical examinations, what makes you qualified to determine if Ms. Jessica Monroe was ,,,,,,,as you put it, violated?"

",,,,Well,,,she said she was, and her clothes were torn off her body."

"Because she said she was? You are here testifying as a witness for the state and all you have to offer is hearsay?"

"Mr. Billingsworth, here in the South, if a lady says she was violated, then she was. Now I don't know anything about where you come from, but down here a lady's word is like gold," she said.

"That may be true Ms. Jackson when it comes to social circles, but not according to the law," he said. "No more questions your Honor."

"You may step down Ms. Jackson," said the Judge. "Do you have another witness Mr. Morgan?"

"Yes your Honor, I'd like to call sheriff Horton."

Billy Ray looked stunned, he didn't know that Mr. Morgan was going to call him as a witness, but he went up and was sworn in anyway.

"Place your left hand on the bible and raise your right hand sheriff," said the court officer. "Do you swear to tell the whole truth and nothing but the truth so help you God?"

"I do!"

"You may be seated."

"Sheriff Horton, tell the court what you saw the night Jeremiah Liggons was caught in the woods after he tried to run away from the crime he just committed. In other words, "What kind of condition was Jeremiah in?"

"Well sir, when I arrived on da scene some of da boys had already captured Jeremiah and dey was a little upset wit him, you know for runnin an all. Dey smacked him around a little bit and started to hang em, but I put a end to dat. I took him into custody, and brought em to jail."

"Where did he get those bruises, and scratches you describe?"

"Near as I could tell, he probably got em from runnin through da woods in da dark, but I cain't be for sure."

"What did his clothes look like?"

"His clothes were torn and bloody."

"Torn and bloody you say? Did they look like he was in a fight with a wild cat?"

"I suppose!"

"You suppose Sheriff?"

Mr. Morgan picked up another brown paper bag, then walked over to the jury, and just as dramatic as earlier, he reached inside that bag and pulled out some bloody clothes, and held them up for the entire court room to see.

"This is evidence number two. These torn. bloody rags are all that is left of Jeremiah Liggons shirt and trousers after Miss. Monroe fought for her life, tearing his clothes and scratching and clawing for survival.

As you can see gentlemen of the jury, these bloody clothes are just as torn and bloody as Miss. Jessica Monroe's clothes. The only conclusion is a simple one, the bruises and scratches Jeremiah Liggons received are the one's he received from Miss. Jessica Monroe," he said. "No more questions your Honor."

"Mr. Billingsworth, you may cross examine."

"Thank you your Honor. Sheriff Horton you testified earlier that my client Jeremiah Liggons was captured by some of the boys and I quote, "Dey smacked him around a little bit and started to hang em, but I put a end to dat," un quote. Now how is it that you can testify under oath that the scratches and bruises my client received came from running through the woods in the dark and not from the lynch mob you call some of the boys?"

"Well sir, I don't rightly know. Some of the scratches and bruises could of come from da boys and some of em could a come from da woods, hell for all I know dey could a come from Miss. Jessica Monroe. I don't know for sure cause I wasn't there," he said nervously.

"That's right sheriff Horton, you were not there, so you don't know what really happened do you? As a matter of fact, you didn't even see the alleged victim Miss. Jessica Monroe until after she was all cleaned and healed, isn't that true sheriff?"

"Dat's true."

"Sheriff, is it possible that there was another man that could of attacked Miss. Monroe, and in a blind angry fury, ya'll went after an innocent man?"

",,,Well,,anythangs possible."

"No further questions your Honor."

"Mr. Morgan, do you have another witness?"

"Yes your Honor, I'd like to call Mr. Monroe to the witness stand."

"Place your left hand on the bible and raise your right hand sir," said the court officer. "Do you swear to tell the whole truth and nothing but the truth so help you God?"

"I do!"

"You may be seated."

"Mr. Monroe, is Miss. Jessica Monroe your daughter?"

"Yes sir!"

"How old is she sir?"

"She's sixteen, sir."

"Sixteen,,,,sixteen. Were you the one that found her screaming in the woods?"

"Yes sir."

"Tell the men of the jury and everyone in the court what you saw that night in question!"

"I found Jeremiah Liggons standing over my baby girl. He had blood on his hands, and my baby girl was laying on the ground all tied up like a hog and she was blind folded. Her clothes were torn off, and her little body was covered in blood."

At that point Mr. Monroe started crying and all the men on the jury looked at me in disgust. The people in the court room started mumbling all around me.

"Order in the court, order in the court," yelled the court officer.

"The next outburst like that and I'll clear this court room," said Judge Parker. "You may proceed Mr. Monroe."

"She wasn't moving, I thought she was dead."

"What did Jeremiah say to you?"

"Dat nigger didn't say nuttin, he jest took off runnin like a rabbit," he said angrily.

"He took off running, is that what you said?"

"Yeap, and if it hadn't been fo some of dem good ol boys over thar," pointing to the jury. "Dat nigger woulda got away."

"No further questions your Honor."

"Mr. Billingsworth, your witness!"

"Mr. Monroe, why did you allow your sixteen year old daughter, to parade around colored men half naked?"

"Dat's a ball face lie. My little girl was pure as da driven snow!"

"I see. Mr. Monroe, when you approached Jeremiah you said he was, and I quote "I found Jeremiah Liggons standing over my baby girl," un quote. Is that true?"

"Yes sir," he said with confidence.

"Where did you say the blood was?"

"On his hands, I seen as clear as day."

"Was there any blood on his clothes, now remember you swore on the bible?"

"I didn't see none on his clothes, but it was sho on his hands, dat's a fact."

"Mr. Monroe, I'm a little puzzled. If my client just finished beating and raping your daughter, then why was he just standing there when you arrived, why didn't he run away before you got there?"

"I don't know, I reckon he ain't too bright!"

"Also, if he did commit such a brutal crime why wasn't there blood all over his clothes and why weren't his clothes all ripped and torn as earlier testimony would suggest?"

"Now don't choo try all dat fancy lawyer crap wit me, I know's what I seen."

"Please answer the question Mr. Monroe."

"I don't know," he said angrily.

"Well I do Mr. Monroe, I do," he said. "No further questions for this witness your Honor."

"Do you have any other witness's Mr. Monroe?" asked the Judge.

"Yes your Honor, I'd like to call Miss. Jessica Monroe to the witness stand."

"Place your left hand on the bible and raise your right hand Missy," said the court officer. "Do you swear to tell the whole truth and nothing but the truth so help you God?"

"I do," she said in a nervous voice.

"Miss Monroe, I know how difficult this must be for to be here, but it's important that you try and remember everything that happened that night, alright!" he said.

"Alright!"

"Now I want you to start from the beginning, tell the court in your own words what happened."

",,,,,It was real hot dat night,,,so I went fo a walk down to da river, I soaked my feet fo a while, den I heard noises in da woods. I thought it might be my brothers playin a trick on me, so I jest sat there acting like I ain't heard nuttin," she said. "Den he grab me from behind, and dat's when I knew it wasn't my brothers, cause he was real strong. I fought em off as best I could and got away,,,,I ran into da woods but he hit me wit a stick or somethin and knocked me down. Befoe I could get up and run he was on my back hittin me in my head. He ripped my dress and covered my eyes wit it, den he ripped some mo and tied my hands, den he turned me over and beat me,,,,,he jest kept beaten me,,," she said as she cried.

"Do you need a break Miss. Monroe?" asked Mr. Morgan.

",,,No sir,,,I can finish," she said as she wiped her tears. "He asked me if I like colored men. He jest kept askin me over and over. Den he ripped my dress open,,,,,and tore off,,,my,,,,,,underpants,,,,,and,,,,,"

All the spectators in the court room gasped out loud, as they watched Miss. Monroe crying up on the witness stand.

"Miss. Monroe,,,I know this is difficult,,,,but can you identify the colored man who raped you?"

"Yes sir," she said as she cried.

"Will you point him out for the court?" She slowly raised her hand and pointed right at me.

"Your Honor let the record show that Miss. Monroe has identified Jeremiah Liggons as the nigger who beat and raped her."

"Your Honor, I object!"

"What are you objecting to Mr. Billingsworth?"

"Mr. Morgan's continued verbal attack of my client, it is prejudicial and leading."

"Over ruled,' said the Judge. "Now sit down."

"Do you have any further questions for this witness Mr. Morgan?"

"No sir, no further questions your Honor."

"Mr. Billingsworth, you may cross examine, and let me warn you again, this here is also a Southern lady, so watch what you say!" the judge warned.

"Yes your Honor. Miss. Monroe, you testified that you were grabbed from behind, beaten from behind, and blind folded from behind, is that correct?"

"Yes!" she said as she wiped her eyes and nose.

"Did you ever see the rapist's face?"

"No!"

"Then how do you know it was my client Jeremiah Liggons, who raped you?"

"Cause,,,,my daddy said,,,he was standing over me,,,when he got there."

"Ah yes, more hearsay," he said sarcastically.

"I ain't gonna warn you again Mr. Billingsworth," said the Judge.

"Yes your Honor. One more question Miss. Monroe, did my client ever tell you his name?"

"No sir," she said sarcastically. "Oh yes, I have one more question. When Mr. Morgan asked you could you identify the so called nigger in the court room, you responded yes, and you pointed to my client Mr. Jeremiah Liggons isn't that right Miss. Monroe?"

"Yes!"

"Miss. Monroe, isn't Jeremiah Liggons the only colored man in this court room?" said Billingsworth.

At that moment, a hush fell over the entire court room like a blanket.

"No further questions for this witness your Honor!"

"You may step down Miss. Monroe. Do you have any further witness's Mr. Morgan?"

"No your Honor, the State rest!"

"Mr. Billingsworth, call your first witness."

"Yes, your Honor. I'd like to call Miss. Debbie McGraw."

The whole court room gasped out loud and started mumbling amongst themselves. They all turned around and watched Mr. Charles McGraw and his daughter Debbie slowly walk into the court room. She walked with her head down and she was holding some wild flowers.

"What's the meaning of this Mr. Billingsworth?" shouted the Judge.

"Your Honor, Miss. McGraw is my first witness."

"Good morning Charles," said the Judge. "I didn't realize you had an interest in this affair," the Judge said nervously.

"I don't particularly enjoy being here William, but my daughter has something very important to say to the court," said Mr. McGraw. "And I trust she will be treated with the utmost respect as my daughter regardless of her condition."

"Of course Charles, of course," said the Judge. "Mr. Billingsworth, call your first witness."

"I call Miss. Debbie McGraw to the witness stand."

"Place your left hand on the bible and raise your right hand Missy," said the court officer. "Do you swear to tell the whole truth and nothing but the truth so help you God?"

"Yes sir, my daddy say's to always tell the truth," she said in a nervous voice.

"How are you doing Miss. Debbie?" asked Mr. Billingsworth.

"I'm fine, how are you?" she asked.

"I'm quite well, thank you for inquiring," he said. "Miss. Debbie, I want you to tell the court what you saw in the woods the day Miss. Jessica was attacked and hurt."

"I was picking wild flowers down by the new church, I always pick flowers down there, see, I picked some today too, aren't they pretty?"

"Yes Miss.Debbie, they are quite lovely. Now try and remember, what else did you see that day."

"I saw Miss. Jessica sitting on the river bank with her feet in the water. My daddy says you shouldn't put your feet in the water because a water snake might bight your toes."

"That's good advice your daddy gives. Now tell the court what else you saw Miss. Jessica doing."

"I saw her running in the woods!"

"Why do you think she was running Miss.Debbie?"

"Cause a man was chasing her in the woods," she said. "I seen it."

"Who was this man chasing Miss. Jessica?" he asked. "Do you know who he is?"

"I don't know his name. Do you like my wild flowers?"

"Yes I do, they are very lovely," he said. "Miss.Debbie, what did he look like?"

"What did who look like?" she said.

"The man you saw chasing Miss. Jessica!"

"He was a big mean man," she said.

"Why do you say he was mean?"

"Because he hit Miss. Jessica with his stick and tore off her clothes. Do you want me to pick you some wild flowers?" she asked.

"Yes Miss. Debbie, I wood like that very much. What did the big mean man look like, was he colored?"

"No, he was white!" she said.

Just then the whole court room erupted into pandemonium. People were talking out loud, standing up and walking out. The Judge was furious.

"ORDER IN THE COURT, ORDER IN THE COURT," the Judge demanded. "Clear the court now, I want everyone out of this court room now,' he shouted.

The court officer quickly cleared the court room of all spectators except the jury, lawyers, witness's, and me. The white folk's went out side and tried to push their way up against the windows to see inside, but the colored folks were not budging, because suddenly they had the best seats in town.

"Would repeat what you said Miss. Debbie?" asked Billingsworth.

"Repeat what?"

"What color was the big mean man you saw chasing Miss. Jessica?"

"White!"

"Are you sure he was white?"

"Yes, I saw the side of his face and his hands, he was white alright. Do you like wild flowers, my daddy likes wild flowers?"

"Yes, Miss. Debbie, I love wild flowers. No further questions your Honor!"

"You may cross examine Mr. Morgan,' said the Judge.

"Miss. McGraw, what type of wild flowers are those you have there?" he asked.

"I don't know, there just wild flowers!"

"How do you know they are wild flowers?"

"Because they don't grow in a garden, they grow wild out in the woods, silly!"

Mr. Morgan wasn't expecting that type of answer, it was obvious that he was expecting to trip her up with that line of questioning, but she didn't fall into his trap.

"How old are you Miss. McGraw?" he asked.

"My daddy says a lady should never tell her age, and a real gentlemen wouldn't ask. Do you like wild flowers, I'll go get you some if you want!"

"No thank you. I don't have any further questions for this witness your Honor."

"Very well Mr. Morgan, Miss. McGraw you may step down," said the Judge.

"Does the defense have any other witness's?"

"No your Honor, the defense rest."

"Very well then, we'll recess until 1:00 this afternoon, at which time we'll hear closing arguments."

"All rise," said the court officer.

I wasn't allowed a chance to talk to Billingsworth, so I never found out why he didn't bring in all the colored gals who had been raped to testify. Maybe he knew best, but why I couldn't take the witness stand on my own behalf, I never knew. Billy Ray took me back to the jail and as we made our way through the crowd. I could see my whole family standing near the court room window. We drove right past them, and momma waved at me and smiled as she stood there in her beautiful yellow dress. Daddy had on his Sunday go to meeting clothes and so did all my brothers and sisters. I got a glimpse of Martin and my sister Cleo holding hands as they smiled and waved at me.

As I drove with Billy Ray back to the jail I was happy, for the first time in a long time I was happy. Miss Debbie saw who the rapist was, and he was white, now I know, they couldn't convict me. Billingsworth turned out to be a pretty good lawyer, and he sure made Mr. Morgan look bad. Later that afternoon Billy Ray took me back to the court house. He didn't say a word to me on the way back, he just took me into the court house sat me down and went to his seat.

"All rise and come to order, the Honorable Judge Parker presiding," said the court officer.

"You may be seated," said the Judge. "Mr. Morgan, your closing arguments."

"Thank you your Honor. Gentlemen of the jury, the state has proven beyond a reasonable doubt that the defendant, Jeremiah Liggons, watched, stalked, and viciously raped Miss. Jessica Monroe, this young, vulnerable, sweet, innocent White girl. She was as pure as the driven snow, until this,,,,,defendant,,, put his filthy ,,,,,,black,,,,,,hands on her. Now granted Miss. Debbie McGraw gave the court compelling testimony, however, with all due respect to her father Mr. Charles McGraw, Miss. Debbie isn't exactly the most intelligent young person in town. It is a known fact that she is in fact a little slow, so with that in mind her testimony should be thrown out. The evidence clearly showed that he is guilty as charged and should suffer the maximum sentence allowed by law which is life in prison with hard labor, thank you."

"Mr. Billingsworth, your closing arguments sir."

"Thank you your Honor. Gentlemen of the jury, what the state has proven beyond a reasonable doubt is it's ability to provide the court with circumstantial evidence. My client, did not, could not, and would not commit such a horrific crime against anyone, let alone a white girl. My client is a college educated man who has lived in this community all his life. Now the evidence shows that he was at the seen, however it does not show he was the perpetrator," he said.

"Our eye witness clearly described the man she saw chasing Miss. Jessica Monroe as a big, mean, white man. My client is a soft spoken, thin, dark skinned colored man.

Miss. Debbie is probably the most credible witness that we've seen today. She doesn't know how to lie, she only knows the truth, and that's all we're all after, the truth. Thank you for your time, the defense rest."

"Gentlemen of the jury, you were given your instructions earlier when you were selected. Now I will send you to the jury room and we'll wait for your decision."

As the jury left the court, I suddenly got a cold chill all over my body. It was the same feeling I used to get when ever I was near the grave yard alone. I didn't know if it was a sign of things to come or if I was just imagining things. Whatever the case, I was scared, I mean really scared. We sat there for about ten of fifteen minutes then we could hear the men in the jury laughing and carrying on. I couldn't imagine what could of possibly been so funny at a time like this, but obviously they found something to laugh about. Approximately twenty minutes after we heard the laughter, they came out and took their seats in the jury box. Then the Judge walked in.

"All rise and come to order, the Honorable Judge Parker presiding," said the court officer.

"Gentlemen of the jury, have you reached a verdict?" asked the Judge.

The appointed jury foreman stood up and looked around the court room and out the window at all the colored and white spectators and said,

"Yes your Honor!'

"What say you?"

"We the jury find the defendant, Jeremiah Liggons,,,,,,,,guilty of rape in the first degree!"

I was stunned as I sat there listening to all the white folks cheering outside. I looked out the window and I could see my momma and daddy. They were crying and upset, daddy tried to comfort momma as best he could, but he looked as though he could barely stand himself. The Judge started pounding on the desk with his gavel to bring the court to order, and I could swear I heard "Dixie" playing in the background.

"Will the defendant rise?" he said. "Jeremiah Liggons, you have been found guilty of rape in the first degree, now it is the order of this court, on June 17, 1937, that you be sent to the Penitentiary of Georgia for the rest of your natural life, where you will do hard labor, and may God have mercy on your poor black soul."

Again the Angel appeared in a bright light and said, *"Be not afraid, for the Lord knows your heart."* "But their gonna send me to prison for the rest of my," life I cried. *"What is prison, but a place to seek and to save those who are lost,"* said the Angel.

Billy Ray took me back to jail and I sat in that cell for two days waiting for him to take me to prison. My momma and daddy came to see me on my last day before leaving and as usual, momma was wearing her pretty yellow dress.

"Don't choo be afraid son, da good Lord's gonna take care a you," said momma.

"Hold your head up high son and always remember who you are," said daddy.

"I can never forget who I am daddy, this old world won't let me," I said. "I going to prison for the rest of my life and I haven't even started living yet."

"Son, da only thang dat matters is da truth, and we knows da truth son. I don't know how I'm gonna do it, but somehow, some way I'm gonna get choo out dat prison, ain't no son a mine gonna be caged up like a slave," he said. "You got my word on it."

"I don't think there's anything you can do daddy," I said. "The Judge has spoken."

"But dat Judge ain't God, even if he thank he is," said momma.

"I want's you to take my bible Jeremiah," said momma. "Read da word like you used to when you was a youngin."

"I can't take your bible momma."

"Yes you can son, you gonna need it more then me right now, besides, I got da word all built up in my spirit," she said. "Da Lord will make a way, somehow, you'll see, jest keep da faith son, and always remember we loves you."

"I will momma, I love ya'll too."

We all hugged for a long time. I closed my eyes real tight, and for a moment I thought I was at home, then I opened my eyes and reality smacked me right up side my head. I took momma's bible and I planned to read it every day. We said good bye and momma and daddy left with their heads held high.

Chapter 15

Prison Bound

When the time came for me to go to the Penitentiary of Georgia, Billy Ray and his deputy came to my cell with shot guns. They looked extremely nervous and they both had sweat dripping from their foreheads. Before I was escorted out of my cell I had a moment to say good bye to Louis.

"Now you make sure you read those books everyday Louis!"

"You mean I get to keep em?"

"Yes Louis, those books are my gift to you!"

"I don't know what to say Jeremiah, ain't nobody never give me no books befoe."

"You don't have to say anything Louis, all I want from you is to know that you will use them everyday, that's all I want!"

"I will Jeremiah, I'll read em till da words fall off da pages," he said with a smile.

"I know you will Louis, I know you will."

We hugged and shook hands after that. I felt as though I was headed for the gallows to have my neck stretched and in many ways, I was headed for a death sentence, even though on paper it was life in prison. We left the jail cell and walked down the long corridor through the maze of colored men and boys. They too were staring at me as though I was headed for the gallows. Nobody said a word and it was just as well because I could read their thoughts on their faces anyway. They looked sad and discouraged, lonely and afraid, and I found myself smiling at them attempting to ease their pain even though I was over run with agony myself. I held my head up as high as I could and walked as proudly as any man could given the circumstances but occasionally I stumbled and my vulnerability came shining through. At that moment I understood how my ancestors must have felt when they were separated from their families and sold from one plantation to the next.

I thought about the power that the white man has over any colored man's life and how he never ceased to yield that power. I learned that justice is blind and the scales of justice are equally balanced, well, to tell you the truth, I think justice takes a peak every now and then, and the scales are unbalanced with the heavy burden that my people carry everyday. When Billy Ray opened the door to the jail house a mob of angry white folks led by Robert Smith, Homer Taylor and David Burns had gathered around the truck.

I suppose they were not satisfied with a life in prison verdict and more immediate justice was in order.

"Ya'll gon home now," shouted Billy Ray.

"Sheriff, all you have to do is turn your back and walk away. Your hands don't have to get dirty," shouted Homer.

"Homer if'in ya'll take one more step in dis direction, your gonna get da first blast of my shot gun," said Billy Ray.

"I know you ain't gonna shoot a white man to protect a nigger," said Robert.

"Yea sheriff, you ain't gonna spill white blood to protect nigger blood!" shouted David.

"I'm only gonna tell ya'll one mo time, go home and let me do my job," yelled Billy Ray as he pointed his shot gun at the mob.

"We ain't never gonna forget dis Billy Ray," someone shouted.

"Nigger lover," said another.

The mob slowly backed up and allowed us to get into the truck. As we drove down the street the mob started throwing rocks and bottles at the truck and the three of us flinched with fear because it sounded like gun shouts. Billy Ray kept on driving through the crowd until we got out of town. When we were all the way out of Burdonville Billy Ray pulled over to the side of the road and got out of the truck and slammed the door. He walked around in circles kicking dirt and throwing his fist into the air. I don't ever recall seeing Billy Ray so angry as long as I knew him. He went on ranting and raving for a while then he started kicking the tires on the truck for a little while longer.

The deputy just sat there looking as surprised as I was. We both sat there sweating like two pigs waiting to get slaughtered. After Billy Ray calmed down he stood in front of the truck and stared at me as if he wanted to shoot me. I didn't know what to do next so I just sat there waiting for his next move. Billy Ray slowly walked over to the passenger door and opened it.

"Get out," he yelled.

"What?" said the deputy.

"You heard me, get out, both of you," he demanded.

"What are you going to do Billy Ray," I demanded to know.

"Either get out right now or I'll drag you out."

The deputy got out of the truck as fast as he could but I just sat there. I didn't know what Billy Ray was going to do or why he was so upset so I just sat there fearing for my life. Billy Ray got even more angry because I wouldn't move so he reached into the truck and grabbed the handcuffs and chains and dragged me out of that old truck. I hit the dirt road so hard I felt like I broke a bone in my back. Dust was all over the place and I couldn't see a thing and when the dust cleared Billy Ray was standing over me with his shot gun pointing right at my face.

"DID YOU RAPE DAT WHITE GIRL JEREMIAH?" he shouted.

"NO!" I yelled. "You know me better than that Billy Ray."

"TELL ME DA TRUTH," he demanded. "DID YOU RAPE DAT WHITE GIRL?"

"I'm telling you the truth," I proclaimed. "You can kill me if you want to Billy Ray but at least I'll die knowing I was an innocent man. Can you live with that Billy Ray, can you live with the fact that you killed an innocent man, a man you once called, friend?"

Billy Ray stood there pointing that shot gun at my face for a few moments then slowly stood up straight. Then he threw the shot gun into the back of the truck, put his hands over his head and started yelling like a mad man. We couldn't understand a word he was saying but I knew that Billy Ray was tormented because deep down inside he knew I didn't have nothing to do with what happened to the Monroe girl. After screaming and yelling for what seemed like an hour Billy Ray stopped and slowly calmed down. Then he turned toward me and slowly walked up to me. With sweat still dripping from his forehead and dust just starting to settle, Billy Ray had a look in his eye unlike anything I had ever seen. It wasn't exactly evil, but it was scary. He didn't blink and for a moment he looked as though he wasn't breathing either.

"If you didn't rape her then who did?" he said with a deep raspy voice.

"I don't know," I said. "I thought you knew."

"You thought I knew what?"

"I thought you knew who raped that gal."

"What da hell are you gettin at Jeremiah?"

"I'd rather not say in front of your deputy!"

Billy Ray paused for a moment as he continued to stare me right in the eyes, then he pointed to the field behind us.

"Go for a walk deputy."

"What!" he said.

"I said go for a walk, NOW," he shouted.

The deputy reluctantly started walking toward the field looking back every few steps and keeping his hand on his gun the whole time. After he got about fifty yards away he stopped and turned toward us and watched us from the field.

"Now, what da hell are you trying to say Jeremiah?"

"Do you remember back when we was youngins and I followed you to Sara James house down in New Bethlehem?"

"Yea, what's dat got to do wit da Monroe gal?" he asked.

"Are you forgettin Billy Ray, I saw what you did to Sara!"

"Are you tryin to say I raped Sara?" he asked. "You don't know what choo talkin bout Jeremiah."

"I may not know what I'm talking about, but I know what I saw Billy Ray."

"You don't know nothin Jeremiah," he said angrily. "If I recall correctly, I tried to tell you that night, but you wouldn't listen, you jest kept beatin on me like a mad man."

"What were you trying so hard to tell me?" I said sarcastically.

"Do you really want to know Jeremiah?"

"Yea, I want to know, tell me!"

"Sara James was my girlfriend. We had been secretly seein each other fo awhile."

"She was your what?" I said with shock.

"You heard me, she was my girlfriend. We had to keep it secret cause,,,well you know why,,so we only saw each other late at night so we wouldn't get caught. I broke up with her when I met Mary."

"Mary?" I said. "Mary who?"

"Mary Houston, we were gonna run away and get married. We knew we couldn't live around here so we planned to live up north, New York, Chicago or somewhere, anywhere but here."

"What happened to Mary, where is she now?" I asked.

"Well, I don't know. The last time I saw her I gave her my gold chain to trade in LaHaye county for clothes, food and train tickets. We were supposed to meet that night in Rosen, but she never showed up. I searched everywhere I could think of, but I never found her. I suppose she decided life would be easier without a white husband."

I didn't know what to say. I was shocked and I didn't want to believe it, but I could tell by the look in his eyes that he was telling the truth. For years I thought Billy Ray raped Sara and he was probably responsible for killing Mary. We stood there staring off into the distance for a while when suddenly a thought occurred to me.

"Hey Billy Ray, do you remember when we was youngins and we made that old raft and pretended to be Fletcher Christian and Captain Blye?"

"This ain't da time for skippin down memory lane Jeremiah," he said seriously.

"Just give me a moment Billy Ray. Do you remember?"

"Yeap, I remember, now what are you gettin at?"

"Do you remember that dead colored gal floating in the river near our raft?"

"Now how you spect me ta forget dat, course I remember!"

"Billy Ray, can you find out if sheriff Banks and old doc Smith wrote a report or took notes on that dead gal?"

"I suppose I could, but what's dat gonna prove Jeremiah, that was a long time ago?"

"Billy Ray, a few weeks back we found Mary Houston!"

"Dear God, where is she," he said with excitement.

",,,,,,She's,,,,,,she's,,,"

"Jeremiah, quit stalling, where is she, I have to see her?"

",,She's dead Billy Ray. We found her remains in the old Sutton place. She looked as though she had been there for years.

At that moment Billy Ray fell down to his knees and started to cry. His deputy came over to see what was going on and Billy Ray motioned to him to go back out into the field and the deputy complied. I helped Billy Ray stand up, because he was obviously distraught.

"We didn't know what to do so we went to see a colored deputy named Penner over in LaHaye county. He took a report, then we took Mary's body home to her family. She's buried over at the old church in New Bethlehem."

"How did she die?" he said as he cried.

"We don't know, but a small piece of your gold chain was under her arm, and her underpants and clothes were torn from her body. She looked as though she fought for her life."

"So you really thought I could do such a thang?"

"Well, to tell you the truth Billy Ray, yes!" I said. "After I found you killing small animals back when we was youngins, and peeking in colored gals windows at night, I thought you were capable of doing just about anything."

"I would never hurt anyone, especially Mary," he said angrily.

"Well somebody did, and somebody raped the Monroe gal, and it wasn't me Billy Ray, I swear to you, it wasn't me!"

"I believe you, but choo been tried and convicted. There ain't nothin I can do cept take you ta prison, I'm sorry Jeremiah, truly I am."

"But there is something you can do, what if the same man killed that colored gal, Mary Houston and raped Jessica Monroe?" I pleaded.

"Ain't no way ta prove dat Jeremiah."

"There is one way Billy Ray."

"What's dat?"

"Old doc Smith," I said. "He examined the dead colored gal, and Jessica Monroe, he can determine if the same man did both rapes."

"Old doc Smith was too drunk to examine da Monroe gal, that's why da Widow Jackson took her in, besides, we don't know if dat colored gal was raped, we was jest youngins remember?"

"Yea, but old doc Smith should know something!" I pleaded. "What about all them colored gals that was getting raped down in New Bethlehem, can't you go talk to them?"

"I reckon, but what about Mary, how do you suppose we tie her in, ya'll done buried her and old doc Smith never did examine her," he said with tears in his eyes.

"I don't know Billy Ray, but at least let's try, please!" I begged. "I don't want to go to prison, and I don't deserve to be there. You owe me Billy Ray."

"I don't owe you nothin, I could of let dat mob string you up?"

"I don't think so Billy Ray, you ain't forgot our blood oath we made when we was youngins have you?" I said as I showed him my right palm.

",,,,I ain't forgot, we made a pact by cutting our right palms wit yo pocket knife and shook hands. We swore right den and there dat we would always protect each other and always keep each other's secrets as long as we lived."

"That's right, and I never told a soul what I saw you do to Sara James."

"Alright, I'll see what I can find out, but I still don't know how it's gonna help you, your still prison bound."

Chapter 16

Life

Betrayal, such an ugly profound word meant to cut deep into ones soul. When I first arrived at the Penitentiary of Georgia, I was met with more hostility and hatred than I had ever experienced in my entire life. They took my momma's bible and I never saw it again. It seemed as though every guard and prisoner knew I was convicted of raping a white girl and they were determined to make me suffer. The first year was the hardest, I was beaten regularly, starved and ostracized. I spent everyday alone, mainly because the other prisoners were to afraid to talk to me because of what I was convicted of, except Big Max. One day while we were standing in the food line, dragging our chains inch by inch, I felt the presence of something large and mean behind me, so I slowly turned around, and to my surprise it was Big Max. He was the biggest and the strongest colored man I ever seen.

"I hear tell you raped a white gal, dat true?" he asked.

"No,,that's not true, I never touched her," I said nervously.

Big Max stood there for a moment staring at me. I thought for sure he was gonna knock the mess out of me, but he didn't. To my surprise he reached out to shake my hand, and I reluctantly stuck my hand out fully expecting it to be ripped off. His grip nearly broke every finger in my hand, but it was unintentional, and we soon became friends. Big Max was in prison for beating up twenty men, at the same time.

The walls were cold and damp, in many ways it was nothing more than a tomb. The sound of bars and chains clanking together had no rhythm or beat, just monotonous and lifeless. Occasionally the sound of a man screaming in agony in a vain attempt to beg for his life could be heard, only to be drowned out by the eerie cry of another man going in sane as he loses his mind. The struggle to maintain faith in a place filled with so much death and pain was difficult at best, yet it was required for all of us who dared to hope and dream of freedom. The battle that waged inside my soul was greater than the war behind those bars, for no man worth a damn would give up that fight.

The isolation from family and friends was like gasping for breath where there was no air, and the lack of a human embrace, just a simple touch, was coveted by all. I was given an old steel sledge hammer with cracks up and down the shaft and I was forced to turn big rocks into little rocks, and little rocks into pebbles, and pebbles into sand. Many times I couldn't tell the difference between my hands and the wooden handle because they were both full of splinters. The rules were simple in prison and I can still quote them today, "Do what your told to do and nothing else, if you want to live." No mail was allowed in or out. The guards made all the rules, and if they were in a particularly bad mood, nobody got anything, needless to say, their bad moods could last six months, sometimes even a year.

It took several years for me to finally come to the realization that I was nothing more than a slave. I was condemned to spend the rest of my natural life in that place. Eating the roach infested food often covered with unknown creatures was a necessity for survival. And I was rarely if ever allowed a chance to take a bath. There was no free time in prison, not even on Sunday. We worked from sun up until sun down. How ironic I thought, my daddy thought I was to scrawny for farm work and there I was working thirteen hours a day. The heat was sweltering, and most men prayed to God for a merciful death, while others moved along like zombies. We wore black and white stripes and we worked chained together at the ankle, forced to move as though we were one man. If there was a weak link he was dealt with quickly by the guards, their whip reminded him to pick up the pace, or suffer even more. One morning while we were out cutting brush and tree's to make way for a new interstate highway, a crow landed near me. His feathers were all ruffled up as though he had been in a cage for a long time.

He looked old and worn out, so I thought he would let me touch him. I reached down to pet him and a shotgun blast rang out. All the prisoners quickly hit the dirt lying still and quiet. I heard a loud voice with a deep southern drawl coming from behind me. "You ain't out here to play wit da wild life," he said. "Now git ta work!" We all quickly got up and started to work, then I looked down where that old crow was standing, and all I saw was blood and a mess of black feathers. I heard snickering behind me so I turned around and saw a snitch named Mooley, he was a white trash prisoner with rotten teeth and a bald head. He was standing unchained next to Mr. Thompson, a fat redneck guard who was sitting on a horse watching over all the prisoners as we worked.

Mr. Thompson, or boss as he preferred to be called had a evil grin on his face. His attempt to hide his eyes behind sunglasses didn't work because I could see right through them. With his shotgun still smoking he smiled as though he enjoyed what he had just done. That fat sonofabitch turned his head and spit some tobacco as if to say to me, that could of been you. By now I had been locked behind those bars like an animal for almost five years and I hadn't heard a word from my family or Billy Ray. As time passed I started to hate him and all he stood for. I started to believe that he had pulled the wool over my eyes with that sad story about how he and Mary Houston were in love. I started to believe that he committed all the rapes and murders in New Bethlehem, and the only reason he didn't kill Jessica Monroe was because she was white. What was the truth? I didn't know if I'd ever find out, and in some ways

I didn't care if I ever did. As we continued cutting a path through the woods we came upon a bee hive. That fat redneck guard thought it would be a good idea if we got some honey for the warden.

"Hey Mooley, run up yonda to da truck and fetch me one dem mason jars on da front seat," he said.

"Yessa boss," said Mooley.

Mooley took off running as fast as he could just like a pet dog. He came back with that mason jar and handed it to Mr. Thompson, but it fell on the ground and shattered. Mr. Thompson was furious and needless to say Mooley was scared to death. He cowered down in fear as Mr. Thompson pointed his shotgun at him.

"You stupid sonofabitch, I oughta blow yo fool head off!"

"I'm sorry boss, I'll fetch you another one boss, I'm sorry boss," he pleaded.

Mooley took off running as fast as he could, only this time when he returned he handed the mason jar to Mr. Thompson with both hands, real slow and careful like. Mr. Thompson looked up and down the row of colored prisoners and pointed at me. "Hey boy!" he said. I ignored him and pretended not to hear him. I just kept working. "Hey boy, I'm talkin to you," he said as he pointed his shot gun at me.

"Me boss?" I said.

"Yea you, boy. Take dis mason jar and fill it up wit honey from dat bee hive ova yonda."

"Yessa boss," I said.

"And you betta not spill a drop, boy!" said Mr. Thompson.

"Dat's right, you betta not spill a drop, boy," said Mooley.

Mr. Thompson and Mooley looked at each other and started to laugh, then Mr. Thompson spit some tobacco right on top of Mooley's bald head. Now all of a sudden it wasn't so funny and Mooley stopped laughing for a moment. With a real sad look on his face he wiped the brown spit off his head, then he quickly started laughing again. By now Mr. Thompson had a serious look on his face and he just stared at

Mooley in disgust. I went over to that bee hive just like I was told and I stood there for a minute as the bee's flew all around me. I was afraid of getting stung, but I was more afraid of getting shot, so I slowly reached down into that hive and pulled out a handful of honey and put it into the mason jar. The bee's were starting to swarm and I could feel their vibration all around my head and arms as they worked themselves up into a frenzy. Big Max stood there staring at Mr. Thompson as if he wanted to kill him. I could see the anger in his eyes and the veins in his neck and forehead looked as if they were about to bust right out of his head.

I looked over to wherer Mr. Thompson was sitting on his horse and I could see him smiling while Mooley kept looking at him as if he were searching for approval. Just as I had finished filling the mason jar several bee's started stinging my arm and fingers. I knew I couldn't drop that jar so I just bit my lip and slowly walked over to Mr. Thompson and handed him the jar full of honey. "Here you go boss, just like you wanted, sa," I said. Mr. Thompson spit that big wad of chewing tobacco out onto the ground then stuck his fat fingers in that jar and scooped up a bunch of honey and put it in his fat mouth. Then he licked and sucked his fingers like he was eating fried chicken. All the prisoners stopped what they were doing and watched. I suppose they were hoping as much as I was that he would choke on that honey and drop dead.

"You sho shapin up ta be a good, boy, ain't dat right Mooley?"

"Yessa boss, he shapin up ta be a good, boy," said Mooley as he snickered.

"Here Mooley, take dis jar a honey and put it in da truck. And Mooley, you betta not spill a drop, you hear?" he warned.

"Yessa boss, I betta not spill a drop, I won't boss."

"How long you been enjoyin these fine accommodations boy?" he asked.

"I was sent here June 17, 1937. That's five years, six months and twelve days, sa!" I said.

"Is dat right, five years, six months and twelve days," he said. "You trying ta get smart wit me boy?" he said angrily.

"No, I was just answering your question, boss," I said with and attitude.

"I don't think I like da way you talkin, you sound kinda uppity. Is you one dem uppity nigga's, boy?"

"Why no sa, I's jest a pow dumb nigga, don't know nuttin bout bein uppity, boss."

Mr. Thompson reached into his tobacco pouch and pulled out another wad of tobacco and put it into his mouth under his tongue. He swished it around then spit. The spit landed on my shoes and I just stood there looking at him. I never blinked and I could see that smile slowly fade from his face. I started to imagine myself snatching that fat white slob off that horse and pounding the crap out of him, but I knew I'd be shot for sure, so I just stared at him.

"I'm gonna keep an eye on you, boy, somethin bout choo don't make sense!"

The next ten years would prove to be nothing but pain and suffering. I learned to become numb in order to block out my feelings, so I seldom thought about my family and friends back in New Bethlehem. After fifteen years in prison I was finally allowed a visit from my family, the year was 1952, but I don't remember the date, only that it was a Sunday afternoon. I was told that only one person could visit, and the visit could only last for twenty minutes. Mr. Thompson called me in from the fields. He sent me to a special yard that had several prisoners on one side of a barbed wire fence, and their loved one on the other side. As I walked along the fence searching for a familiar face, I saw momma. And for the first time in my life my mother looked old. Her hair was white as snow, and her skin was cracked and wrinkled. The only thing that was the same was her grace, poise and dignity. She still walked with her head held high and she was wearing that pretty yellow dress she always wore to church and for special occasions. As I approached the fence I could see momma's big brown eyes swell up with tears.

"Momma," I cried.

"Hi baby," she said.

"How are you momma?"

"I'm fine son, how are you?"

"I'm doing just fine momma."

"How they treatin you son?" she asked. "You look tired!"

"As well as can be expected momma," I said. "That's enough about me. How's daddy and the rest of the family? Tell me everything, I want to know it all."

"Didn't you get my letter's son?"

"No, ma'am, we ain't allowed to get no mail," I said. "What's wrong momma."

"Not allowed to get mail?" she said surprisingly. "You cain't write either?"

"No, ma'am!"

"Dear Lord, all dis time we thought you was just to ashamed to write. Jeremiah,,,your daddy passed away fifteen years ago, son," she said as she hung her head and started to cry.

"Right after they took you away, his heart just couldn't take it no mo, we wrote and told you."

I reached up and grabbed the fence and tried to hold my momma's hand.

"Get yo hands off dat fence boy," Mr. Thompson yelled out.

"Yessa boss, sorry boss," I said. I tried my best not to cry but I couldn't hold back. Even though it had been fifteen years since daddy passed away, it seemed like that day, to me. My knee's were suddenly weak and it was hard to stand up. I couldn't believe it, my daddy was dead and he never saw me leave this place. Momma quickly changed the subject because we were short on time.

"Martin and Cleo got married," she said. "They have four boys. They named their oldest son Jeremiah, and Martin is the school teacher back home."

"That's great momma, that's great."

"Your brother Abraham got married to Annie Mae, they got three little girls and they all talk just like they momma, always in somebody else's business."

"What about James, Kathyren, Mark, John, Mary and Lula?" I asked.

"All of em married except Mark. He say he ain't got time for no foolishness," she said with a smile.

"What about youngins?"

"Well, lets see. James and his wife Winnie got one little boy. Kathyren and her husband Nathaniel got three girls and a boy. John and his wife Samantha don't have any youngins yet. Mary and her husband Samuel got six youngins and Lula and her husband Jim got seven youngins"

"Woooeeee," I shouted. "That's a whole lotta grandchildren momma."

"Your brothers still works da land. We was able to save up enough money to buy it from Billy Ray."

"Billy Ray?" I said. "That land don't belong to Billy Ray, it belong to his daddy."

"His daddy died about ten years ago, son, and Billy Ray sold two hundred acres to us, dirt cheap."

"Is that right?" I said. "Is he still the sheriff momma?"

"Yep, but not for long," she said. "He's running for mayor of Burdonville, and it look like he gonna win."

"Now don't that beat all. Momma, what about old doc Smith, is he still alive?"

"Yea, but he ain't no doctor no mo. He just sit's around da barber shop with da rest of them old fools, chewing peanuts and telling lies. Why you ask about old doc Smith Jeremiah?"

"No reason momma, I was just talkin," I said with sadness.

"Jeremiah, we know you innocent son, and yo daddy knew it too! Yo daddy loved you so much son and he never ever doubted that one day you gonna be free!"

"I know momma, but it don't look like that's gonna happen."

"Hush wit dat kinda talk," she said firmly. "Da good Lord gonna set choo free, you just wait and see."

"But, momma, it's been fifteen years."

"It don't matter if it's been fifty years. Da Lord may not come when you want Him, but he's always right on time, you hear me.'

",,,Yes ma'am," I said in a whisper.

"Speak up, I cain't hear you,"

"Yes ma'am."

"Now, that's betta. Now don't choo ever give up on da Lord, and I promise He won't ever give up on you!"

"Visiting time is over," a guard yelled.

"Momma I have to go now," I said hurriedly.

"Pray son, keep praying. Da Lord hear's you, jest talk to Him. You hear?"

"Yes, ma'am, I will," I said.

"Always remember I love you son, we all loves you!"

"I love you too momma," I said. "Tell everybody, I'll be home directly!"

"Dat's da spirit son, dats da spirit. Teach somebody somethin in here son, you is a teacher or have you forgotten?"

"How momma, how can I teach men that don't want to learn?"

"How do you know dey don't want to learn, have you asked dem? Bye son."

Momma stood next to that fence until all the guards rounded us up and sent us back to the field to work. While I was working I could see momma and all the other people walking down that long dirt road headed for home. I watched her until that bright yellow dress disappeared in the dust and shadows. I didn't know it then, but that was the last time I would see my mother alive. Doing time was hard, but doing life, was harder! I thought long and hard about what my mother said. Later that day, I asked the warden for permission to teach some of the prisoners to read and write in our spare time, and surprisingly he said yes, I suppose he was getting soft in his old age.

He supplied me with burnt sticks to use as pencils and some scrap paper. Big Max was my first student, and it wasn't easy. The guards didn't like me teaching the colored prisoners to read and write, and they often made it difficult by turning off the lights so we couldn't see, but we pressed on anyhow, starting with the ABC's. It was very challenging, but we slowly made progress. Soon I was teaching more and more colored men things they had never known before. For a time, I felt like I was a free man in a real classroom, and soon I was teaching math, English, and a little science,.

Chapter 17

The Confession

I once heard a man say confession is good for the soul, if that's true, then what about the damage done before the confession, who is that good for? In 1957 a new warden was appointed to the Penitentiary of Georgia. He was a young white man, short in stature, and not more than forty. He wore the same black suit everyday, with black patent leather shoes that were so shiny, he could see his own reflection in them. His thick black framed glass's always slipped off his nose and he was constantly pushing them up with his right index finger. He had a nervous twitch in his left eye and he was always smiling and talking to himself. He was full of ideas for the prisoners like, group therapy, church on Sunday morning, regular visits from family, and recreation to ease stress. The prisoners had never heard of such things and the guards were equally baffled.

Many guards quit or transferred in protest, but the prisoners thought he was to good to be true and were slow to respond to his ideology. Most thought that he wouldn't last, and felt as though it didn't make much sense to get used to something that wouldn't be around very long. Most prisoners were accustomed to harsh treatment, bad food, and pain. Anything else, was strange. On June 1, 1957, we were hit with a terrible storm that devastated most of the south. Tree's were up rooted and thrown all over the fields by the strong winds, and homes of all shapes and sizes were completely demolished. The rain came down in buckets day after day, and the flood waters destroyed what ever was left by the winds.

The bodies of cows, horses, mules, chickens, hogs and dogs were floating through the streets, dead and bloated. Homeless farmers were clinging to wood and debris struggling to survive as the storm continued to rage with no end in sight. I prayed the storm would destroy the prison walls, but no such luck. Those walls were solid and strong. The prison was elevated on a hill and it didn't appear as though the flood waters would cause much of a threat, but as the flood waters continued to rise, the warden ordered every man to fill sand bags and place them around the walls and entrance of the prison as a precaution.

As we worked in the wind and rain, hundreds of homeless white farmers came to the prison for refuge. They stood at the gate with their only possessions and demanded entrance. Their clothes were ragged, muddy and soaking wet. What a sight, I thought, white folks demanding to be let into prison. The warden was stuck between a rock and a hard place.

It appeared as though he didn't have any place safe enough for those white women and children amongst all the murderers and rapist, and at the same time he didn't want to turn them away. So he decided to put all the murderers and rapist in make shift tents out on the recreation yard. We were ordered to take our blankets and sheets with us, even though we knew it wouldn't be enough to really protect us from the storm.

The white homeless men, women and children were then taken to our cells. He ordered a complete lock down while our guest were with us, and needless to say, we weren't happy. Especially those of us who had to move out into the wind and rain soaked yard. Several prisoners were sent out near the flood waters to get wood and debris so we could burn it to keep warm, and our food was cooked over that same open fire in a large cast iron pot. I never thought I'd want to be inside those cold dark walls, but I was wrong.

The water continued to rise and more and more homeless farmers and their families were arriving everyday, which meant more and more prisoners were sent out to the yard, even if they were not murderers or rapist. We had been out in that yard for almost two weeks, and three or four prisoners came down with pneumonia and died. They were stripped down to their drawers and their bodies were placed in a shed out back. Their prison clothes were sent to the laundry and their boots and blankets were passed out to other prisoners who needed it. With all the white families taking up space in the prison, I couldn't believe not one single colored family came near the prison. I suppose history and two hundred years of slavery was enough of a deterrent not to ever come near a prison. They probably decided to fight out the storm on their own and take their chances.

I started to worry about my family and all the folk down in New Bethlehem. We weren't allowed any news papers and we didn't have access to a radio so I didn't know if the storm and flood waters affected them. When a white farmer passed by me on his way into the prison I asked him.

"Excuse me sa," I said. "Have you heard any news about Burdonville and New Bethlehem?"

"Da flood water didn't go dat far east boy," he said. "Why, you got kin folk down there?"

"Yes sa, my momma and brothers and sisters!" I said with pride.

"Seem like nigras always get lucky," he said. "All da good white folk I know, got wiped out," he said as he put his head down and turned away.

He quickly went into the prison to get out of the rain, and I just stood there and smiled. That was the best news I'd heard in a long time. Suddenly, all the rain, wind and cold didn't seem to matter that much anymore, all I cared about was that my family was safe. Soon the rain stopped and the flood waters started to recede, and it wasn't long after that the homeless farmers and their families started to leave the Penitentiary of Georgia. It wasn't long after that that life was back to normal.

We went right back to work, only this time we were ordered to burn the carcass's of dead farm animals and clear the roads of debris. On June 18, 1957, I saw a long black car drive up to the prison. I couldn't see who was driving that car, but the guards quickly opened the gate and let that car drive through. Shortly after that I was ordered to report to the wardens office. Just before I got to the building I saw that long black car drive up to the gate. Those guards quickly opened it and that car left as fast as it came. When I got to the wardens office, a guard told me to wait outside.

I had no idea what was going on and I was afraid it was bad news about someone in my family. After waiting for an hour or two, the warden called me into his office. He was sitting alone behind a huge mahogany desk with pictures of his wife and kids on it. There was a picture of the president on the wall behind him, and the flag of the United states was standing in the corner.

"Are you Jeremiah Liggons?" he asked.

"Yes sa, boss," I said nervously.

"I'm warden Peabody, Jeremiah. Have a seat. Do you know why I called you in here?"

"No sa, boss."

"Jeremiah, I read your file. It says that you are an educated man. You earned a Bachelor of Arts degree in Education, from Scripture college in Atlanta back in 1937. So you can stop all the yassa boss talk," he said with a smile.

"Yes sir," I said as I sat up in my chair.

"I was just delivered some very important documents and a very important letter that might be of great concern to you."

"Who is the letter from Mr. Peabody?" I asked.

"I think you should just read it first," he said as he handed me the letter.

I sat there for a moment staring at the blank envelope. I was nervous and almost to afraid to open it, but I knew I had to. What could it say, and who was it from, I thought. Maybe it was bad news about momma, or one of my sisters or brothers. Naw that couldn't be it, even this warden wouldn't call a prisoner in for that type of bad news. Well, all I could do is open it and see what ever it is, I thought.

Dear Jeremiah,

It has been many years since I last saw you. I never meant to hurt you or cause you any pain, but as it turns out, I did. I'm dying of cancer Jeremiah and the doctors say I only have a couple of days left. Before I go on to meet and stand before the Lord in judgment, I must confess to all the horrific crimes that I committed over the last thirty years. In 1923, I found a young colored gal walking through the woods all alone. She was beautiful and had long pretty black hair she kept in a pony tail. We talked for hours and she told me that she was running away from home because she was tired of working on her daddy's farm. She said she planned to go to California to find work in the picture shows. We talked and laughed as though we were old friends. Suddenly I felt a strong desire to kiss her, but she pulled away. That made me angry, so I grabbed her and forced her to kiss me. She started hitting me as hard as she could but that only made me more furious, so I beat her, and ripped her clothes off her body, then I savagely raped and strangled that poor child. I knew what I did was wrong, but Lord forgive me, I couldn't help myself. I was so afraid of getting caught, I quickly carried her naked body down to the river and threw her in.

You weren't supposed to be involved, I didn't think anyone around New Bethlehem would ever find her, especially because that old river was so dark and full of debris, besides I thought, she wasn't from the area and nobody would notice she was gone. Shortly after that, I realized how much I enjoyed the power I had over another human life, and I wanted to experience that power again. So one night I decided to go into New Bethlehem and find a victim. I approached several homes until I finally found young teenage girls alone in their rooms. They knew who I was and they were not afraid so I told them that if they don't let me have my way with them I'd make all kinds of trouble for their family. They were usually reluctant, but they always complied. One by one they started having babies, my babies and they knew they couldn't tell, so they claimed some unknown man snuck into their rooms and attacked them. I didn't have to kill any of them because they never struggled, fought or screamed. I had complete control and all the power. One day I was walking down Old Miller road and I came across young Mary Houston. She was dressed in a pretty pink dress and her hair was braided as fine as can be. She was one of the many young colored gals I was having my way with, but she was a little more strong minded than the rest.

I asked her where she was going and she told me none of my business. I grabbed her arm and demanded to know where she was going and she refused to tell me so I slapped her face. She still didn't want to tell me so I dragged her kicking and screaming to the old Sutton place. She fought like a wild cat and almost got away, but I managed to knock her unconscious, at which time I tore her pink dress off and raped her. As I committed this terrible crime she woke up and started fighting again, and this time I strangled her to death. I was to afraid to move the body, so I just left her there, hoping it would be years before she was found. Before I left the old Sutton place I found Mary's diary in her purse. She wrote about all the times I had my way with her, the dates, times and places. She even wrote about some of the others. I decided to keep it, why, I don't know, but I did. I continued to have my way with young colored gals over the years, until young Jessica Monroe and her family wondered through New Bethlehem. Late that afternoon while all the colored folk were heading home after working on the new church and school. I saw young Jessica Monroe walking down through the woods near the river, so I followed her. She went and sat on the muddy bank and put her feet in the river.

Her clothes were ragged and her private parts were always exposed, so I lost all control. I couldn't help myself, I had to have her no matter what. I knew the sound of the river rushing by would mask any noises I made as I quietly snuck up behind her. I wasn't about to let her see my face, so I snuck up behind her and struck her over the head. She quickly got up and ran through the woods, bumping into tree's and bleeding from her head. I quickly caught up to her and wrestled her to the ground, and covered her eyes. She fought, and screamed, but she wasn't strong enough to get away. I beat her until she was unconscious, then I ripped the rest of her rags off her body and raped her. I asked her over and over did she like colored men. I begged her to tell me she did, but she only grumbled. When I finished raping her, the rag over her eyes had come off, and her eyes were wide open. I thought she was looking at me so I started to strangle her. That's when you showed up. I ran into the woods to hide and I watched you as you stood there in shock. When her daddy came up behind you, and you took off running into the woods, I knew right then and there that you would be blamed. While Mr. Monroe chased you through the woods I started to go back and finish strangling her to death, but she stood up and managed to stager back to the church. Young Debbie McGraw told the truth when she testified at your trial.

She saw everything. She thought I was a white man, and that was always to my advantage. I'm sorry for what I did, and I'm sorry for letting you waste away in prison for a crime I committed. I gave the new sheriff, Mary Houston's diary as proof and evidence and I told this story to Mayor Horton, in hopes that you would be freed. He promised to take this new evidence to the Governor of

Georgia, on your behalf. And finally, I must also confess the secret that has helped me to betray so many colored folk and white folks alike. I'm really a white man. I have lived my life as a colored man for over forty years. It was out of guilt and shame for all the atrocities that my people have committed against your people over the years, and I thought I could help to improve the colored man's life style and living conditions by teaching school and preaching as a colored man. Colored people were always so trusting and nobody ever asked me where I came from or who I was. Everyone just assumed I was a light skinned colored man, and they welcomed me into their lives with open arms. Please find it in your heart to forgive me.
Sincerely,
Reverend Hightower

I couldn't believe it, I didn't want to believe, but there it was, in black and white. I never in my life felt so angry. This man baptized me, taught me how to read and write, gave me books, helped get me into college and spent countless hours with me and my family, eating dinner and fellowshiping. I was betrayed, used, abused, disrespected, beaten, lied too, convicted of a crime I didn't commit, and to top it all off, I was taken away from my family for twenty years. The Reverends death bed confession may have been good for his soul, but, I don't know if it will be good enough, to set me free, I thought!

"This other document is from the Governor of Georgia, signed and sealed. It was delivered by the Mayor of Burdonville, Mr. Billy Ray Horton. It appears as though you have some very good friends in very high places, Jeremiah," he said.

"It appears so, warden."

Chapter 18

I'm Negro American, I'm Angry and I'm Here

After I left warden Peabody's office, I was escorted by a guard to my cell. I was like a zombie and I couldn't hear anything or anyone around me because I was still stunned and in disbelief about Reverend Hightower. I laid down on my bed in a fetal position and started to cry like a baby. After a while I fell asleep, and it was probably the best sleep I had in twenty years. When I woke up I could see the moon light shinning in through the window and I stood to get a closer look. The Angel appeared in my cell right behind me and said, *"The Lord has delivered you from bondage because of your faithfulness. Now it is time to go home."* "Go home?" I asked. "What home do I have to go to?" *"Open your eyes Jeremiah, and go forth and proclaim the Lord's goodness. Home is where you make it,"* said the Angel. When the Angel disappeared I picked up a pencil and paper, then I sat on the floor and started to write. I wrote an essay that I call "I'm Negro American, I'm Angry and I'm Here," It is an essay about life as seen through my eyes, however, I'm not controlled by all that I see.

I'm Negro American, I'm Angry and I'm Here

I'M NEGRO AMERICAN

Though I am but one man, my hopes and dreams are no different than any other. But my fears and frustrations can only be seen through mine own eyes. For over 400 years my people have watched and waited with great anticipation of that elusive day, when we could truly be called "Free men." Though steel shackles have long been removed, they've been replaced by despair, welfare, drugs, hopelessness, poverty, racism, and hate. I've seen other races lay in the sun risking skin cancer just to get darker. Wow, isn't it wonderful to be born with beautiful brown skin, thick full lips, and dark brown eyes. How ironic! The color of my skin was once enough reason to lynch a man, now it seems to be "acceptable." Maybe I'm idealistic, but wouldn't it be nice if we could celebrate our differences instead of separate ourselves from one another.

As a Negro American man living in a society that does not treat all it's citizens fairly, I wouldn't want to live anywhere else, because despite its many flaws, I can still dream a free mans dreams. Don't get me wrong, I'm not content with all these injustices and racism that still persist today, I simply believe that if we as Negro Americans can learn to unite, bring back family values and push education, we can begin to make a free mans dream come to pass. I remember a time when extended family was as equally important in raising children as having an immediate family. If an extended family member saw me doing some "dirt," I would get my butt whooped, and by the time I got home, I got another whuppin. Growing up, I often got into trouble which led to a whuppin. I know I deserved it sometimes, but I'd like to think I was completely innocent, most of the time.

My family is very important to me, and I believe they are the back bone to my success as a human being. When I was a little boy in New Bethlehem Georgia, I remember an old church down a long, dirt country road, where I could hear the sound of the choir through the woods. I remember the church graveyard with graves dating back to the early

1800's. When I stood near the graveyard, I couldn't help but think of all the history that land holds. In that graveyard behind that old church is buried slaves, former slaves, service men, house wives, children and free men. The stories they'd tell would fill a library. The knowledge and wisdom that is buried there is overwhelming. That's why we must honor and respect our elders while their with us, because what they have to offer can't be found in any books. They could teach us things about being Negro American that we've never thought of. During my time in prison I learned that teaching is my gift, and my imagination is my escape, and more importantly, Jesus is my redeemer.

When I was young I tried to imagine what it must have been like to work seemingly endless hours from sun up until sundown in the blazing heat and freezing snow, no pay, no gratitude, very little clothing and shelter, and with death the only guarantee of freedom. Where pain and suffering are constant companions, to be bread like cattle and sold much the same. Whipped, beaten, lynched, raped, and murdered, the only comforts were old Negro spirituals, beautiful songs of prayer and praise with hidden messages of hope and whispers of freedom. I often imagine what it must have been like to live in a land that my people walked for thousands of years where the air was fresh and the water was pure. I imagine an open air classroom where every day and night was a lesson of education and survival. Living among nature and dwelling in its riches and glory. To study plants and animals that one day might save a life and calculate the stars in the firmament.

Where generation after generation, pride, dignity, loyalty, and honor are passed down like a golden baton, precise and oh so accurate! I'm Negro because my ancestor's blood flows through my veins. It warms my body and softens my heart. I see the golden sunsets as I stand on the shores of the motherland. I hear the sounds of music and rhythmic drums in the distance. I feel my brothers and sisters pains and joys so far away across the ocean. Kings and Queens are in my family tree, I'm told. I walk with pride, dignity, and I command respect. I'm American because my Negro ancestors blood was shed against their will. Though we tilled the ground and picked the cotton, freedom was not at hand. We fought in wars in order to earn our freedom and show our patriotism. We marched in sweltering heat and heavy rain. We were lynched, raped, beaten, and thrown in jail, simply because of the color of our skin. Through it all, we persevered and are still overcoming. I was born here, as was my father, his father and his father before him. Negro American, "yes," I am!

I'M ANGRY

Who was it that promised, "Forty acres and a mule?" Why are the prisons filled with my people? Why do police officers stand above the law they are supposed to up hold? Why does there seem to be two sets of rules, one rule for them and one rule for us? Does "Black on Black" crime just happen, or is it a grand design? What do drugs, alcoholism, and death have in common? Are gangs really fighting each other, or are they waging war inside themselves? Is it true what they say, that an Negro American man must be twice as good just to get the same job? Is racism taught, or do racists instinctively hate? I wonder! Am I alone with my questions?

Maybe so, there doesn't seem to be many answers! Anger is an emotion that we all have in common at one time or another. Sometimes it's under control and at other times it's out of control. I'm angry because Lewis Latimer, Garrett Morgan, Dr. George Washington Carver and countless other Negro American inventors have not been given their rightful place in history nor the respect and recognition that they deserve. I'm angry because the Buffalo Soldiers, Tuskegee Airman and many, many other servicemen fought bravely and died valiantly in war to uphold the American dream, and are seldom recognized for their honorable exploits. I'm angry because this society chooses to call Bonnie & Clyde legends, and Billy the kid and Jessie James folk heroes, when they were quite simply ruthless thieves and murderers. At the same time, cowboys like Bill Pickett and Nat Love went basically ignored. Pickett invented the sport of "bulldogging" which is still in existence today in major rodeo circuits across the country.

I'm angry because many Negro Americans helped to settle the west and history has chosen to forget their contributions. I'm angry because so many great minds were lost at the hands of hate and racism. So many great minds were lynched, burned alive, shot, beaten and thrown in prison in many cases, for crimes they didn't even commit. This country has truly been cruel in the past, has anything changed? I'm angry because the media often exaggerates the news when a Negro American is supposedly involved in a crime. Every channel repeats over and over the report that says "A Negro man is wanted by police in connection with this crime." "A Negro was seen at the scene of the crime and police want him for questioning." They use the word "Negro" like it's a dirty word, and it's something that should be spit out when said.

I'm angry that so many people who don't even know any Negro Americans think we're all either thieves, murderers, gangsters or sexual predators. I'm angry when my brothers and sisters talk Negro American pride, then turn around and stab another brother or sister in the back. I'm angry because often times my people copy other peoples cultures and don't fight to maintain our own. I'm angry that it's easier to get a divorce than to get help. I'm angry because white women clinch their purse when I get to close or quickly lock their car door when I approach. I'm angry that so many people view Negro Americans as entertainers and happy go lucky. I'm angry that there are so many liquor stores, illegal guns and drugs in the Negro American community. I'm angry that this country spends more money to send people into space to explore the unknown, rather than on cancer that we know kills millions of people world wide.

I'm angry that family values have been replaced by careers, wealth, and material gain. I'm angry that child molesters and rapist don't get the same treatment in the justice system as murderers, such as life with no parole. And why not, they leave behind victims who are traumatized for life. Some victims never recover, others become abusers themselves, while some become productive citizens despite their pain of the past. I'm angry that so many wild animals are endanger of extinction because man hunted them for sport, such as the Buffalo, tigers, lions, and countless others. I'm angry that the rain forests and jungles are slowly disappearing. I'm angry about pollution and waste. I'm angry about hunger, starvation, homelessness and crime. I'm angry because many of our elderly citizens are cast aside into convalescent homes and often forgotten. I'm seriously angry, however, "under control."

I'M HERE

It's a fact, I'm here and I must be reckoned with. I'm here because for over 200 years my ancestors were kidnapped from their home, shackled from head to toe, thrown into the belly of wooden ships, packed like sardines with the dead still shackled next to the living and taken thousands of miles away to be sold into slavery. I'm here because it's my God given right. I'm here because I was born here and it is my constitutional right to be here. I'm here because so many millions and millions of my people lived and died in conditions worse than those of farm animals. I'm here because so many greatly known and unknown Negro Americans gave their lives freely in order that we all might be free. I'm here, and my ancestors have been for over 400 years. I'm a citizen of the United States. I'm here with all the honor, respect and splendid glory of Kings and Queens. I'm here, and whether anyone chooses to see me or not, doesn't matter, because I know who, what, and where I am, so it's a fact, "I'm Here."

Yes, I'm here, maybe I'm your postal carrier, doctor, lawyer, politician, neighbor, police person, public transportation driver or perhaps I'm your teacher, gardener, service repair person, or preacher. I might be a scientist, inventor, professional athlete, actor, salesperson, contractor, engineer or housewife. I could be a writer, singer, dancer, business person or friend. I could be all these and much, much more. I have many shapes and sizes, I'm many shades of brown, I enjoy the theater, walks on the beach, picnics, swimming, boating, camping and hiking. I love the stars in the night, sunrises and sunsets. I love family reunions, traveling to new and exotic places. I love to love and make love and I enjoy horseback riding. I have friends and enemies. I put my pants on one leg at a time, I cry when I'm sad and laugh when I'm happy. Does any of this sound familiar.

We all have so many things in common and at the same time we are so different. Everywhere people go, everything they do and whatever they see, they will ultimately have to reckon with me. I'm on the television, radio, newspaper, billboard, magazine cover, and I'm on their minds. I'm part of the past, I'm part of the present, and because this is my country too, I'm an even larger part of the future. So get used to it, "I'm Here." I was conceived in love, born into a family filled with warmth, love and compassion, then thrust into a world that is filled with hate. I wear my beautiful brown skin like a badge of honor even though some call it a curse. My psyche is constantly challenged on many different levels, such as, "will I be pulled over by the sheriff and harassed for no reason or will I be mistaken for someone connected to a serious crime or will I be denied employment, housing or other opportunities because of the color of my skin. My examples are just a few, but the situations are many and ongoing.

I'm not paranoid, just realistic and I do believe one day things will change for the better. I've learned to stay focused by not allowing the circumstances of life to change my goals and I remind myself of the thousands of contributions that my people have given to the world. I remind myself of all the sacrifices that my ancestors and my parents made on my behalf. Such as the 400 year struggle for freedom during the slave era or as I like to call it, the hostage era. I call it the hostage era because a slave never puts up resistance and a hostage is someone who is captured, kidnapped and continues to strive and fight for freedom. This nations dirty past is filled with death, deception and pain which in turn catapulted Negro Americans into the world spotlight, thus, exposing many hidden demons that lurk in the depths of human oppression. I'm Negro American, I'm Angry & I'm Here.

Chapter 19

Now Comes Freedom

On June 19, 1957, at 7:00 a.m, warden Peabody released me from the Penitentiary of Georgia with a full pardon. It was a hot humid morning and I was released at the same time as Big Max. I was wearing the same old clothes I was wearing when I first arrived. They were still raggedy, and they were still to big, but I really didn't care. When they opened the gate, we didn't hesitate to step through. Once we were on the other side of that barbed wire gate, we stood there for a moment looking down the long road ahead. My first instincts were to run, but I held back. I fell to my knee's and thanked God for delivering me from bondage. Big Max fell to his knees right next to me.

"Dear Lord," I prayed. "Thank you for delivering me from the hands of the evil one. Thank you for keeping me safe and strong, during those times I started to doubt your love. Guide me safely home dear Lord, and help me to find my place in life. Watch over all the men in that place I just left Lord, many of them are just as innocent as I was. In Jesus name I pray, Amen."

After I prayed, we stood up and I saw the Angel watching over me just as she had always done, *"It's time to go home,"* she said. Then we started to walk, then we started to walk a little faster, then we started to jog, then we started to jog a little faster, then we started to run. I never looked back, not even for a moment, I just ran, and ran until I couldn't run no more. As we slowed down to catch our breath, we started to notice all the remains of farm houses and barn's that were left over from the storm earlier in the month. We walked for miles and miles through one ruined county after another. As the hours passed, we found ourselves in areas that were not as devastated as the ones we had just passed through. We saw farmers out working, and children were playing. Several more hours passed and I started to find myself in familiar surroundings. As we walked down the road I thought about the symbolism of being set free on June 19.

"Hey Big Max, do you know what to day is?" I asked. "Naw, I don't believe I do Jeremiah." "It's June 19," I said with pride. What's so special bout June 19?" he asked. "Well, I'll tell you what's so special about June 19. For over 90 years Negro Americans all over the country have been celebrating a special holiday called Juneteenth. The celebration of freedom is what juneteenth is all about. Juneteenth, or June 19, 1865 marks the date when many of the slaves throughout the country learned they had been freed. To give you a broader understanding of what life was like for a slave, we must take a trip back into history. Slaves were beaten, lynched, burned alive, mutilated, raped, sold like cattle and shot for attempting to escape. Families were separated and sold for profit. Life as a slave was difficult at best, working day after day in the scorching sun or freezing cold as well diggers, canal diggers, black smiths, furniture builders, home builders, field workers who planted and tended crops.

They were mammies who were responsible for taking care of their owners children as well as cooking and cleaning. Slave girls and women were expected to satisfy their owners perverted sexual desires in what ever manner demanded. However, if a female slave refused to have sexual relations with her owner, she would be beaten and raped until she learned to submit upon demand. Slaves wore rags for clothing and only ate scraps or slop from the owners table. If they were lucky they might be fed a potato, rice and bread. Slaves were considered to be livestock not human beings, so if a slave was injured in any way shape or form the only medical treatment received was from a Doctor who ordinarily treated sick horses and cows. For decades now the movie industry in Hollywood has portrayed slaves as wide eyed, scared, grinning, stepen fetchen, yassa boss, happy go lucky weaklings. In fact, the slaves were hard working, intelligent, cunning and all about survival. They developed a communication system that was capable of sending messages all over the country side right under the unassuming owners nose. The communication system consisted of what was commonly referred to as "Old Negro Spirituals."

These spirituals were sung by the slaves who were working in the fields and could be heard by other slaves working in other fields on other plantations. Songs such as "Go down Moses" which was a message for runaway slaves traveling on the underground railroad with Harriet Tubman who was also known as "Moses." Or "Follow the North Star" which was a song that gave directions to runaway slaves. Then there was "Freedom land" a song that would give hope and inspiration to those who would dare run for freedom. Though many slaves dreamed of freedom few knew how to obtain it. Men like Nat Turner, Denmark Vesey, and Gabriel Prosser are but three who decided that they would rather die than be slaves.

They each led rebellions in the south which led to the death of some of their owners as well as themselves. After more than three hundred years of slavery, President Abraham Lincoln's Emancipation Proclamation went into effect on January 1, 1863. The Emancipation Proclamation freed only those slaves in the states fighting with the Union. Slaves in other states such as Texas were not informed of their freedom for two more years. Not until June 19, 1865 when General Gordon Granger of the Union army arrived in Texas, more than two years after slavery was officially abolished would Texas learn that the slaves were free. As the news spread throughout Texas and other states, Negro Americans celebrated.

Festive foods such as roast hogs and steers were prepared, music was played, and people danced and sang.

After Negro Americans were freed, they began a long and arduous journey toward equality and respect. More than ninety years later, courageous men and women are still fighting for freedom civil rights, equality and respect. Juneteenth is a day of celebration and remembrance for all those millions of slaves who never knew freedom until death, and for all those who lived to see freedom and paved the way for Negro Americans today." Big Max had tears rolling down his massive face, and he didn't wipe them away. I felt like a free slave as I walked down that old road and I'm sure Big Max felt the same. As we approached a fork in the road Big Max said,

"This is where we part ways old friend."

"Thanks for everything Big Max," I said with sadness. "What's your real name?"

"Maximilian, but they call me Big Max because the warden said Maximilian was to much name for a Negro," he said. "Good bye Jeremiah Liggons."

"Good bye,,,,,,,,,,, Maximilian." We shook hands, and went our separate ways.

Chapter 20

Home Sweet Home

As I continued to walk, I came upon a sign that said, Welcome to Burdonville. I approached Burdonville with great apprehension. I wasn't sure what to expect as I walked through town, but I was determined to walk through with my held held high as my momma and daddy always taught me. The first place I saw was the old jail. It was the same as I remembered it, old and in need of paint. The new sheriff was sitting out front chewing tobacco and reading the newspaper. I don't think he ever noticed me walking by, because he never lifted his head.

Shortly thereafter I saw old doc Smith sitting in front of the barber shop with several other old white men. They just stared at me as if they didn't know who I was. When I got near the train station, the old white station attendant was out front sweeping the porch. He stopped and stared at me as I walked by, and I never nodded or acknowledged him in any way, and I'm sure he didn't know who I was anyway. Mr. Timble was stacking boxes in front of his grocery store and just like the station attendant, he didn't even know who I was.

I walked a little further and I was shocked to see, young Jessica Monroe standing in front of the town bar with several young white men all around her. She had thick makeup on, and she was wearing a short skirt and cowboy boots. Those white boys had their hands all over her and she appeared to be enjoying every minute of it. She noticed me passing by, and she stopped smiling and stared at me in disbelief. I kept walking never saying a word to her, and soon I was out of town. There it was at last, I thought, Old Miller road. Now I knew I was almost home. Old Miller road was no longer a dirt road, but a paved street.

The old homes that dotted the country side were a little bigger and most were painted in bright colors, like white or yellow. There were white picket fences in some front yards, and chain link fences in others. I walked down Old Miller road right past the place where the old Sutton place used to be, and I stopped and paused for a moment. I continued down the road until I came upon the new church and school. The school had several attached rooms on either side and it was painted bright red, and right out front in big bright white letters it read, "Horton School." The church was just as beautiful, with white walls and pretty stained glass windows, and a tall bell tower in the front.

I walked around to the back of the church to search for daddy's grave. When I found it, I started to cry. His headstone read, "Beloved Husband & Father." I knelt down to touch that marble stone. It felt strong and solid, just like daddy was. When I stood up, I noticed there was a fresh mound of red dirt, with flowers just starting to wilt next to daddy's grave.

When I looked at the headstone I was shocked to see that it was my momma. She had just passed away, and just like daddy, I never got to say good bye. I fell back down to my knees and cried like a baby. When I finally got up enough strength to stand up, I noticed her head stone, which read, "Beloved Wife & Mother." The two most important people in my life were gone, and even though I had eight brothers and sisters, I felt completely alone. I stood there next to their graves for a while, thinking about all the good things my momma and daddy taught me and all the fun I had growing up. I found myself smiling, then laughing. Momma wouldn't want me to be sad, especially because I knew her and daddy were in heaven with the Lord.

I started to walk down to that old river, when I heard laughter, singing and talking. It was coming from a small playground down the road. I took a closer look and I could see all my family, as well as the church folk having a picnic. They all looked so grown up and prosperous. I felt like I didn't know them anymore and I didn't know how I was going to fit in. I went down to the river and sat down on those red muddy banks just like I used to do when I was a youngin. Suddenly and without any warning, I heard a familiar voice.

"I see you got my package, Jeremiah!"

I didn't have to turn around, I knew who it was, I'd recognize that voice anywhere.

"Yeap, I got it," I said. "What took you so long?"

"Well, these things take time," said Billy Ray as he sat down next me.

"I reckon."

"What choo gonna do now Jeremiah?"

"I might run for Mayor of Burdonville, I ain't decided yet," I said sarcastically.

Billy Ray and I started to laugh and hug, then he paused for a moment when he saw I wasn't laughing. Mayor Liggons has a nice ring to it, I thought.

"Well, when you decide, I'll be over yonda wit yo family and the other church folk celebrating Juneteenth. They've been waitin along time to see you old friend," he said laughingly.

"I'm just gonna sit here and enjoy my freedom for a while, I'll be over there directly."

"Good enough," he said. "Hey, Jeremiah, welcome to home sweet home!"

Home sweet home, anything was better than prison I thought. Billy Ray walked over to the Juneteenth celebration and I sat and thought about my future. I never had a girlfriend, so marriage wasn't in my immediate plans, that's for sure, but I sure would like to meet just the right kind of woman, someone like my momma, someone that's kind, gentle and spiritually minded I suppose. As I sat and thought to myself, the Angel appeared just as she always had when I was about to do something stupid. *"Be patient Jeremiah, the Lord will send you your perfect mate, just be patient and wait on the Lord,"* she said.

She's never been wrong before, so it's about time I started listening to what she has to say. So I'll just sit here under the bright blue southern skies of Georgia, on these red banks of the Ginsburg river, swatting flies and swamped by unbearable heat and humidity and be patient. I'm enjoying the first day of freedom in nearly twenty years. Not much has changed in this place we called New Bethlehem, a place not likely to be found on any maps, it is quite simply, the colored part of town.

The end!

Made in the USA
Las Vegas, NV
06 September 2021